VENOM BLADES

BLOOD TIDE

BOOK TWO
BY RICHARD SLADE

*To Stuart & Janette
Enjoy!
From Richard Slade
:)*

First published in Great Britain in April 2014

Second edition published July 2014

Copyright Richard Slade 2014

Dedicated to my biggest fan, Michelle Mason.

Introducing...

This story includes a rich tapestry of different characters. Here's a quick guide to the Blades family:
- Edward Blades - Our autistic and highly intelligent main hero. When aliens attacked his school he led his classmates to stop them, and now leads a team of alien fighters. His codename is 'Venom'.
- David Blades - Edward's father. David is an invigilator in exams at Edward's school, and often makes terrible jokes.
- Sarah Blades - Edward's mother. Sarah is a councillor representing Pinchbeck, and is very practical and assertive.
- Emma Blades - Edward's teenage sister. Emma spends most of her time at boarding school, and is considered much cooler than her brother.
- Sophie Blades - Edward's youngest sister. Sophie is a larger-than-life figure who makes friends easily and dotes on her brother.

These are the different members of Edward's heroic team, the Blade Runners:
- Lily Kilgour - A confident, flirtatious French beauty, who is protective of her twin sister, Abbie, and is the leader of the Blade Runners' Beta team. Her codename is 'Viper'.
- Abbie Kilgour - Lily's timid twin and a member of the control team, based at the Blade Runners' headquarters. Her codename is 'Queen Two'.
- Nick Spartan - A friendly, confident and loyal member of the Beta team. His codename is 'Boa'.
- Cathy Jones - Edward's caring and brave best friend, who is now his second-in-command in the Alpha team. Her codename is 'Asp'.
- Bob Underman - A tall, humorous member of the Beta team. His codename is 'Savane'.
- Luke Tucker - Bob's best friend and a clever member of the Beta team. His codename is 'Keelback'.

- Amy Frederickson - A friendly, lively member of the Alpha team. Her codename is 'Harlequin'.
- Beth Archangel - A moralistic and tactical member of the Alpha team. Her codename is 'Cobra'.
- Robbie Liddel - A popular, easy-going and wise member of the Alpha team. His codename is 'Adder'.
- George Knight - A member of the Alpha team, who is disliked for his crude sense of humour and his treatment of Amy when they were dating. His codename is 'Splitjaw'.
- Emily Buzzer - A bright, enthusiastic, morale-raising member of the control team. Her codename is 'Queen One'.
- Carter Guinness - A gentle giant and member of the control team. His codename is 'King Two'.
- Harold Vandaleur - An extremely intelligent tactician, who is in charge of the control team. His codename is 'King One'.
- Sky Jennings and Tasia Close - An inseparable pair of quiet, hardworking Beta team members. Sky is unusually tall, while Tasia is quite short. Sky's codename is 'Copperhead', and Tasia's codename is 'Lyre'.

Then there are the villains of the piece, the vampires:

- Viktor Korbachev - The leader of the vampires.
- Rose - A bloodthirsty recently-transformed vampire.
- Dave 'Rossy' Ross - An unusual vampire.
- Sickle - One of Korbachev's most fearsome henchmen.

And some innocent bystanders:

- Kirsty Sheppard - A teenage girl who gets caught up in the vampire invasion.
- Ivy South - Kirsty's friend, who is also caught in the vampire attack.
- Janine South - Ivy's mother, who is continually disappointed in her daughter.

Prologue

It was raining in the field, and the sheep had fled into their stable to shelter. The grass had long since been drowned in mud, and not even the dimmest, most naïve of the lambs would try grazing in this weather. As the rain continued to pound, two figures trudged across the swampy land.

The taller of the duo was a young man, broad-shouldered with lean, muscular arms, almost seven feet tall, obviously a powerful figure. He wore black combat trousers and a hoodie, and had an angular, mean-looking face and a shock of white-blond hair, gelled into spikes, under his hood. The second, smaller figure was a teenage girl, slight, innocently attractive and far less threatening in her appearance. She was about five and a half feet tall, with long scarlet hair, and she wore a light grey hooded fleece and blue jeans.

"How are you holding up?" the man asked in a strong German accent, not sounding as if he particularly cared.

"I'm *starving*," the girl hissed in reply, licking her lips, her harsh voice contrasting with her unimposing appearance.

The man stopped suddenly, sniffing the air.

The girl looked at him, frowning. "What are you doing?"

"Getting lunch," he responded shortly, as his head slowly turned in the direction of the sheep shed. He grinned as he looked back at his teenage companion.

"Fancy some lamb chops?" he sniggered.

***

They dumped the bodies of the sheep in a nearby river, and continued their journey, still licking the blood covering the lower halves of their faces.

"Nearly there?" the girl asked.

The man nodded. "I smell humans. We can't be far off."

They reached the top of a hill, and the young man laughed. "There we have it!"

* * *

"We apologise for the delay, ladies and gentlemen; we appear to be dealing with some technical difficulties. Fear not, for we'll be back on the move again shortly."

Clare was annoyed. She had finished work late because the restaurant in London was short-staffed, and all she really wanted was to get back to her flat in Bromley and see her boyfriend. Now the train had decided to stop in the middle of nowhere.

As the steward who had just spoken passed her seat, Clare reached out and tapped him on the arm. "Sorry, do you know how long it's going to be?"

The steward gave her a brief grin. "Don't worry, madam, it should only be a couple of minutes!" he told her in the same cheerful tone he had used a moment ago, before heading back to the driver's cabin.

He was careful not to let his smile fade and the worried expression hidden beneath show until he was out of sight of the passengers.

Clare checked her phone again, and was frustrated but not particularly surprised to find that there was no signal.

Great, she fumed inwardly. *I'm stuck in the middle of nowhere, with no way of contacting Tom to tell him I'll be late. Just fantastic.*

Staring out of the window in boredom, she saw a number of figures dressed in black hoodies and combat trousers approaching the train.

Clare blinked. The figures were gone by the time she opened her eyes.

So, on top of everything else, I'm cracking up now, as well.

* * *

The steward had checked with the driver, and there was nothing wrong with the power lines feeding electricity to the train. None of the emergency stop levers had been deployed either. The train had just decided to stop, without warning or reason.

Frustrated, he leaned out of the window, only to see a teenage girl in a grey fleece standing by the rails, looking up at him desperately.

"Please, let me in," she begged. "It's really horrible out here. I'm soaked; my friends are soaked; we just want to shelter somewhere. Please."

The man's heart filled with compassion for the poor girl - she couldn't have been much older than sixteen. "Sure, sweetheart," he said soothingly. "You and your friends can come in."

"Danke," a sinister voice said behind him.

* * *

Clare had almost nodded off when the screaming started.

It came from the driver's cabin, out of the blue: a loud wail of human pain. Clare almost jumped out of her skin, as did most of the other passengers. She exchanged a panicked glance with another passenger sitting across from her, but then the doors on either side of their carriage slid open and dark figures poured in, pouncing on passengers and stewards alike.

As people began to scream, Clare scrambled out of her seat, her nostrils filled with the tangy metal scent of blood. Her brain struggling to process what her eyes were telling it - because they couldn't be real, these creatures that looked like humans but were tearing people apart in an animalistic way; they just could not be real.

A tsunami of gore washed over the floor of the carriage. Terrified passengers were scrambling for the emergency exits, only to be cut off by the attackers. In desperation Clare looked around for a way to escape, to see an enormously fat man swing an emergency axe at a nearby window, which disintegrated. Without thinking twice, Clare lunged out of the window after the fat man, landing heavily on the ground.

She struggled to her feet, trying to ignore the cuts and bruises she had just gained, and ran - but she only got as far as the top of a nearby hill, where a man with spiked blond hair blocked her path.

"No running for you, plain Jane," he hissed mockingly, glaring straight into her eyes.

Clare froze like a rabbit caught in headlights, as a wave of numbness spread through both her body and her mind. She was utterly immobilised, completely helpless; unable to look away from the man's blood-red eyes.

I've been hypnotised, she realised calmly.

The man stepped towards her, licking his lips.

"Dinner time," he sniggered, a look of glee on his face.

Then another figure moved into Clare's line of vision - a teenage girl with shockingly red hair. She blocked Clare's view of the blond man, but she still couldn't move.

The damage is already done, she understood. *I can't escape.*

There was a childlike longing in the teen's voice as she pleaded with the man: "Please, Sickle. She'll be my first human blood."

The blond man - 'Sickle' - sighed, before responding in an exasperated tone, "Oh, all right, then."

The girl spun round to face Clare, giggling and clapping her hands together with excitement.

Her eyes were the same shade of crimson as Sickle's, and they blazed as she stepped closer to her prey, opening her mouth wide.

Instead of canines, there were two long, wickedly sharp fangs.

Those fangs were the last things Clare ever saw.

Chapter 1

Cathy Jones kept thinking the same thing: *Why the hell did I sign up for this?*

She was sitting perfectly still on a sofa, in the middle of a huge warehouse. Not far in front of her, directly in her line of vision, was a desk, at which her friend Harold Vandaleur, a lean seventeen-year-old with dark brown hair, now sat. On top of the desk was set of computer screens and a master keyboard, which Harold was tapping away at, and speaking into a microphone attached to a headset he was wearing. Sitting at the chair to the left of Harold was Emily Buzzer, her blonde hair cascading down her back as she tapped at her own keyboard, staring intently at the screens above her as they displayed different information. On the chair to the right of Harold was Abbie Kilgour, apparently doing the same as Emily. Abbie's long black hair was tied back, but occasionally Cathy noticed her reach up and impatiently flick a loose strand out of her face. Above the desk was a clock, which clearly said that the time was half past nine at night.

Cathy had had plenty of time to analyse her surroundings, because she hadn't moved a muscle in at least fifteen minutes. Her entire body was frozen, with the exception of her eyes and their lids (thankfully, because that meant she could still blink to stop her eyes drying out), and, annoyingly, her brain. She was extremely bored, she was getting fed up with the sole company of her own thoughts, and her nose was itching. *Why did I volunteer for this?* she asked herself furiously. *Why didn't I just let Edward test his stupid 'venom blades' on someone else?*

Edward Blades was a close friend of Cathy's (and, briefly, her boyfriend, though she decided after five days that they were better off as friends). Until nearly four months ago, they had led relatively normal lives - they went to St. Jude's Academy in Bourne, they had a group of good friends and they were preparing for their A level exams. Then one day their school had been frozen out of time with only Year 12 inside it, and they had to fight off an army of alien predators and their calculating masters, the Gorakdezors. The Gorakdezors were mutant refugees from a destroyed planet: they had travelled to Earth in search of new bodies, and had chosen to abduct a group of Year 12 girls to transplant their brains into them, as they were most compatible with the Gorakdezors' original forms.

Thankfully the school they attacked happened to have a headmaster with experience of fighting aliens, and though he wasn't on hand to help, Edward knew his secrets - the computer program on the headmaster's computer containing details of trillions of different alien species, and the stash of weapons hidden behind fake walls in his office. Best of all, Edward was an obsessive fanatic of *Doctor Who* and other sci-fi, and this - combined with his brilliant memory - had made him a born leader, as he modelled his leadership skills on those of the Doctor and other television heroes. With Edward guiding them, the Year 12s had successfully wiped out the attacking predators before destroying the Gorakdezors and their mothership, though several of the teenagers had died in the process.

But that wasn't the end - because the headmaster, Oliver Ludgrove, had cottoned on to Edward by then. Having realised the Year 12s knew the truth about him, Ludgrove resigned and moved away, but before he left he gave Edward a key fob which would allow him to access a warehouse containing tons of salvaged alien technology, as well as computers capable of hacking anything - other computers, phone lines, and even entire satellites.

After recruiting Cathy and fourteen others who had fought against the Gorakdezors, Edward set up a team to fight other alien or paranormal threats, with Ludgrove's huge warehouse as their base. Splitting the group into three units - two teams of six to go out into the field, and a team of four to stay at base and watch over operations as their 'control' team - he called the team his 'Blade Runners', a name he took from his surname and his trademark weapon. This was a dagger with a golden handle shaped and decorated to resemble a snake, with a blade imbibed with venom capable of paralysing a human being for around fifteen minutes. Edward had two of these, and both were also parting gifts from Mr. Ludgrove. It was later Harold's idea for everyone in the team to have snake-based codenames, to link with Edward's weapon of choice.

However Edward still only had Ludgrove's word that the venom could paralyse people for that long, and he wanted to test it in controlled conditions. This was why Cathy, a member of the Blade Runners' 'Alpha Team', was now sitting on a sofa in the team's base, immobilised with a scratch on her finger where she had cut herself on the blade, and an extremely itchy nose.

At least she could still hear what the others were saying up ahead. The rest of the Blade Runners were out in Bourne Wood, dealing with an alien incursion - not the first the team had had to deal with since they officially opened for business, nearly three months ago.

"King One to Venom, are you receiving me, over?" Harold was saying rapidly into his mic.

Edward's voice came back over the loudspeakers connected to the computer. "*Venom receiving, King One. Give me the blip's position, over.*"

"Blip within a thirty-metre radius, Venom. Keep scouting, and remember: shoot first and ask questions later. This thing's packing heat: whatever it's got as a weapon, there was barely anything left of the victims; just ashes. Over," Abbie added hastily.

"*I'm well aware of what happened to the victims, thank you, Queen Two,*" Edward replied testily. "*Concentrate on tracking that radiation signature instead of telling me what I already know, over.*"

Abbie flinched a little. "Sorry. Over."

If she could move, Cathy would probably have stormed over to the console and yelled through one of the mics at Edward to stop being so obnoxious. But, of course, she couldn't.

This latest alien incursion had been discovered twenty-five minutes ago, when the Blade Runners' equipment had picked up a radiation surge on the outskirts of Bourne Wood - the equipment couldn't identify the type of radiation, which meant it must have been a long way from home. Just as the team were about to follow up on it, Emily intercepted a phone call from a few yards away from the surge: a woman was screaming down the phone at the police, telling them that a short blue-skinned man had just incinerated her boyfriend. A second later Abbie detected another surge in the same spot, and the call cut off.

Edward and the rest of the Alpha Team had immediately headed off to Bourne Wood, following a continuous trace of a residual version of the radiation Abbie had detected. Cathy would have gone too, but she had volunteered to be the subject of Edward's venom experiment and so she stayed behind with his spare dagger.

"You're almost on top of the bugger now, Venom," Harold told Edward. "Just a few yards away... no, the other way..."

At this point the effect of the venom wore off so suddenly, Cathy nearly fell out of her chair with shock. "Jesus *Christ*!" she shouted, fumbling on the sofa next to her for her stopwatch and holding it up.

"Seventeen minutes and forty-nine seconds," she declared, before dropping the stopwatch and beginning to frenziedly scratch her nose.

∗∗∗

The alien was a Mekrashi named Cassadant, and he was very scared.

He was fifteen years old in human terms, and had been joy-riding a stolen space pod across the solar system with a couple of mates when a solar flare hit. His mates had been atomised almost instantly, but his craft had been badly damaged and had spun towards Earth. Cassadant had crashed on the outskirts of Bourne Wood half an hour earlier, armed only with a standard issue Sun Force Globe (no Mekrashi ever left home without one) and thanking the forces of the universe that his pod's shielding tech had still been active, preventing the impact from being that serious or the human authorities from detecting him.

But his panic had increased significantly when he encountered two humans, a male and a female, and in desperation he incinerated the man, before running after the woman and killing her two minutes later. More scared than he had ever been in his life, Cassadant had charged into the forest and had been running for the last twenty minutes or so. His mind was racing too, thinking of anything and everything that could happen to him on this strange planet.

What he didn't expect to happen was for a black leather figure to leap out of the shadows and tackle him, pinning him to the ground. But of course, that was exactly what happened.

"Stay down," the lean figure growled through what a human would have recognised as a motor biker's helmet, unsheathing a dagger and holding the blade against Cassadant's throat.

Another figure, short but powerfully built and also dressed as a biker, came into Cassadant's line of vision and stood over him.

"Venom," the second figure said urgently. "King One says Asp came round after seventeen minutes forty-nine."

"Cool," 'Venom' said shortly. "I'll deal with this one; you find his weapon."

"Please," Cassadant stammered. "I- I don't want any trouble, I didn't want to come here... It was an accident; please don't hurt m-me..."

The second man kicked Cassadant hard in the side. "Was it an accident when you murdered two innocent people?"

"Please!" Cassadant whimpered. "I didn't know... I thought they were going to hurt me!"

"What's your name?" the first figure barked, still holding him down.

"C-Cassadant."

"And your species?"

"Mekrashi."

"Where's the weapon you used to kill those people?"

"In my pocket..."

The second figure crouched, slipping the device out of Cassadant's pocket. "What is it?" he asked, studying the glowing orange orb.

"Sun Force Globe," Cassadant explained. "Every Mekrashi owns one... Got to be able to defend ourselves..."

"Splitjaw, get it back to base," Venom ordered. Splitjaw nodded and moved away swiftly.

Venom leaned closer to whisper in Cassadant's ear. "Listen, I know you're scared, and I know how worried people will be about you, and I know you think I will hurt you. But it'll be a lot worse for you if our government finds you. They'll torture you, dissect you... It's better this way." With that, he climbed off his captive and stood up. "Come on, sit up."

Gasping with relief, Cassadant sat up. Venom moved behind him.

"It's better for you if it ends quickly," he said, drawing a silenced handgun and quickly shooting Cassadant in the back of the head.

Chapter 2

"All ready?" Robbie Liddel, an imposing dark-skinned young man, asked from the driver's seat of a Sports Utility Vehicle.

Edward nodded as he opened the passenger door. "Yeah, the body's loaded in the back, and Splitjaw's got the weapon."

"I'll give him a hand with it," Beth Archangel said, her red hair flying loosely around her shoulders as she jumped out from the passenger seat, manoeuvring round Edward, and went round to the back of the vehicle. She, too, was in biker gear (minus her helmet), which was a ruse to prevent the Blade Runners from being identified while out in the field.

The short, stocky George Knight was walking back to the SUV with the Sun Force Globe in his gloved hand. As Beth approached, he glared at her from behind his visor.

"I came to help you," she explained shortly.

"I can manage," he replied in a bitter tone, before pulling the back door of the SUV open and stepping inside. He was greeted by Amy Frederickson, who avoided eye contact with him as he got out the strong box and put the spherical weapon safely inside.

Those three had history. George had dated Amy for nearly three months before the Gorakdezor incursion, but cheated on her with Lizzie Bader, a classmate, and later dumped her. During the Gorakdezor incident Beth had told Amy about George and Lizzie's affair. The fact that Amy and Lizzie had been friends, and that Lizzie had died during the fight with the Gorakdezors, meant neither Amy nor George were ready to confront each other properly afterwards, and had skirted around the issue ever since Edward recruited them both into the Blade Runners.

"Once we work out how to operate the Sun Force Globe we can use it to deal with the Mekrashi's body," Edward told the rest of the group.

"Should we get back to base?" Robbie asked as they all got into the SUV.

"Nah, I need to get back to Pinchbeck, it's my sister's birthday do and I don't want to miss it. Drop the strong box and the Mekrashi back at the warehouse and then head home; Harold'll call us if we're needed."

*＊＊

"Happy birthday to you, happy birthday to you!" Edward sang as he strode into the Red Lion pub, his large mop of brown hair preceding him into the restaurant area. "You're fifteen years old today, enjoy your GCSEs!"

His dark-haired sister Emma, the birthday girl in question, gave him a withering look. "Thanks, dear brother," she said in a sarcastic tone, standing up to awkwardly hug him.

Edward responded by giving her a huge wet kiss on the cheek. She squirmed and backed away. "Ewww!" she shuddered.

"Love you too," Edward laughed, sitting down next to his father David, who looked a lot like Edward but balding and portly, and who appeared amused at Emma's discomfort. David was an invigilator in exams at Edward's school, which had earned Edward a sort of credibility with other students - or at least among those who had never heard David speak, as Edward constantly asserted.

"Be nice to your brother," their severe-looking mother Sarah told Emma, looking insincere as she once again attempted to resolve the old argument. "He's just trying to be affectionate."

"I don't like public displays of affection; he knows that! He's just trying to make me uncomfortable!"

"It *is* your birthday, Emma," David pointed out with a smug grin. "You may have to get used to people being affectionate to you."

"Yeah, Em," Sophie, the youngest Blades sibling, unnecessarily put into the conversion. Emma scowled at her. Sophie stuck her tongue out at her elder sister.

"All right, enough," Sarah said wearily. "Can we all try to get along on Emma's birthday please? No arguments, no sticking tongues out at each other, no scowls. Just be *nice* for once."

"I was trying to be," Edward protested, but Sarah gave him a sharp look, signalling that the conversation was over.

Looking around, he noticed the TV in the corner of the bar room, visible through an open door behind the bar, was switched on and showing ITV News. CCTV footage was being shown of several people in biker gear, and the newsreader could be heard saying, "*There is still no new information on the identities of these mysterious vigilantes. However some eyewitnesses, who do not wish to be identified, have encountered these vigilantes on occasions, and the majority of their stories reveal that these mysterious figures refer to themselves as 'Blade Runners'...*"

Edward smiled, pleased at the continued safety of the team's identities - the biker ruse had been Emily Buzzer's idea, and had worked a treat. Though he suspected she had only mentioned the idea because her boyfriend Robbie Liddel thought she looked good in leather.

"Do you want to play Mario Kart with me?" Sophie asked Edward.

Edward shrugged. "Why not? Dad, did you bring my DS like I asked?"

"Yes, son," David sighed, getting it out. "Though why you can't look after your own belongings I don't know."

"I was in Bourne all day! I didn't want to have my DS in the car where someone could nick it. Em, are you playing?"

"Nah, let Dad play instead," Emma replied. David looked pleased as she passed her DS to him.

"I think I'm finally getting the hang of this game," he told his children smugly, switching the DS on.

"I'll still pound you, old man," Edward laughed.

"Me too," Sophie pointed out.

Sarah smiled. "Face it, David, you'll never beat them. The kids are just too good, and you are just too old."

David looked wounded. "You're only six months younger than me, darling," he reminded his wife.

"Yes, but I am under no illusions that I'm rubbish at Mario Kart."

"Not as bad as him," Edward remarked, and everyone laughed.

***

The streets of Pinchbeck were relatively quiet now, as it was now around ten at night and the sky was dark. People were either at home or at bars, celebrating Saturday night.

A thick cloud of black smoke moved quickly across the sky, before whirling and converging on the roads. The smoke manifested, transforming into solid bodies. As the dark cloud faded, suddenly an empty street was filled with about twenty people - nearly all wearing entirely black clothing.

A gaunt man stepped forwards, his dark hair slicked back and his hands outstretched. When he spoke, it was with a thick Russian accent.

"Time to raise an army," he hissed.

Chapter 3

"Ooh, I put on my shoes, and I'm ready for the week-eeeeeend!" three teenage girls sang badly, laughing hysterically as they paraded through the aisles of the Spar.

Happy, relaxed and already rather drunk, though it was only half past ten, the girls were at a party a few streets away with a bunch of friends. They had volunteered to go to the Spar to stock up on more crisps and alcohol.

"That was *mental*," Annabelle Black giggled, almost tripping over her own feet. She was a tall, painfully thin girl with jet black hair, which combined had earned her the nickname 'Emo Girl' - because people were really unimaginative.

Ivy South, who in contrast to her friend was short and full-figured with white-blonde hair, nudged her. "Yeah, and I can't believe you got off with Michael Shawn! He's *well* fit!"

"You can talk," Annabelle replied. "How many guys did you get off with?"

Ivy sniggered. "I lost count after the first twelve."

The third member of their party, Kirsty Sheppard, laughed along with the other two, but her heart wasn't really in it. At just under sixteen years old, Kirsty was a short, slim girl with chocolate-brown hair and olive skin. She was two years younger than Ivy and Annabelle, and was not as used to wild parties. She had a growing sense of unease, particularly about how much her friends had had to drink so far.

Ivy seemed to notice something was up, and put her arm round Kirsty's shoulders. "Hey, Kirst. You don't have to hang out if you don't want to..."

Anxious not to be seen as the baby of the group, Kirsty quickly shook her head. "No, I'm all right."

"But if you're not enjoying yourself..."

"I'm fine," Kirsty interrupted, knowing she was trying to convince herself as much as she was trying to reassure Ivy.

Ivy shrugged. "All right, then." Then she gave Annabelle a sneaky glance, and said quickly, "Bagsy I'm not buying the beer!"

"Bagsy me neither," Annabelle added.

Kirsty groaned. "Oh come *on*, I'm underage! I'll get done if I try to pay!"

"You've got a squeaky-clean record though," Ivy pointed out. "If you do get caught, the worst you'll get is a slap on the wrist and a lecture."

Annabelle grabbed a six-pack of Fosters and pushed it into Kirsty's hands. "Off you go then."

Kirsty looked from one of her so-called friends to the other desperately. "I can't believe you're making me do this."

"I can't believe you're taking so long to get it over with," Ivy replied impatiently. "We could be at the party by now!"

"So, *go*!" Annabelle ordered, spinning Kirsty in the direction of the till and giving her a push in the small of her back.

Off-balance, Kirsty staggered forwards a few steps, before steadying herself by grabbing the edge of a freezer full of frozen food.

Straightening up, she walked anxiously up to the till, resentful thoughts directed at Annabelle and Ivy filling her mind all the time.

Surprisingly, there was no-one behind the till. Putting down the cans of beer, Kirsty leaned awkwardly on the desk and waited.

Now she came to think of it, she hadn't seen any staff in the Spar since they came in, a couple of minutes ago. Even then, there had only been an old guy at the till, and he now seemed to have vanished.

Just as Kirsty was beginning to get annoyed, a door at the end of the middle aisle opened, and a blond-haired man wearing a Spar T-shirt strode out.

"How can I help you, young lady?" he asked politely, a Germanic edge to his accent.

Kirsty nervously held out the money to pay for the beer. "Can I buy some beer, please?"

His eyes narrowed. "You're a little young, aren't you?"

Kirsty cursed inwardly.

The man shrugged. "Ah well. I like 'em young."

Then two screams came from the back of the shop.

Kirsty almost jumped out of her skin, spinning round in horror - and felt two powerful arms grab her around the waist.

"Go on," the blond man snarled in her ear, his accent suddenly stronger. "Struggle. I love it when they fight back..."

Panicking, Kirsty launched a barrage of desperate punches at her attacker, all of which seemed to bounce off with very little effect. Laughing, he pinned her to the desk, before looming over her like a spectre of doom.

This cannot be happening, she thought briefly. *This can't be real.*

Then she saw the blond man's mouth open wide, to reveal two wickedly-sharp fangs.

"Time for a bite to eat," he said darkly, before leaning closer, his fangs pointed towards Kirsty's neck.

What? This definitely *can't be real.*

There was a sudden explosive sound like glass breaking, a huge impact on the back of the man's head, and then his eyes rolled back and he slumped off Kirsty, onto the floor.

Ivy stood over her, holding what was left of the wine bottle she'd smashed into the blond guy's head.

"*Vampires*, Kirsty!" she shrieked.

Kirsty was too shaken to reply, but did consider that Annabelle was nowhere to be seen.

Then three huge men - vampires - charged out of hiding, up the aisles towards them.

"*Run!*" Kirsty screamed, and the two girls ran for the door out of the Spar - only to see another vampire, a young woman, waiting in the doorway, fangs bared.

Kirsty pulled Ivy away from the door, and they both sprinted for the door the blond man had come out of only a few minutes earlier. Kirsty reached the door first, but looked back to see that Ivy had tripped over her heels and was now at the vampires' mercy.

"Kirsty! *Help*! *HELP ME*!" Ivy bellowed frantically, as the four vampires closed in around her.

More scared than she'd ever been in her life, Kirsty threw herself through the door and slammed it behind her. Trying to ignore Ivy's panicked screams, she took in her surroundings - she was in a dark room, and in front of her was a granite staircase leading down to a cold stone cellar.

Knowing she had only a few seconds to hide before the vampires caught up, Kirsty took the steps three at a time, and ran across the stock-filled cellar. She crouched behind a huge crate, filled with boxes of all kinds of food, and held her breath, trying to keep quiet.

About fifteen seconds later - the most nerve-racking fifteen seconds Kirsty had ever lived through - the door opened, and heavy footsteps sounded on the stone floor.

"Come out, come out," came a deep voice. "I know you're in here..."

Silence.

He laughed. "Not going to make it easy for us? Ah well, we know you can't escape. Consider yourself saved for later."

Then the door slammed shut, and there was an audible click as it was locked from the outside.

Half-hyperventilating, Kirsty pulled her mobile out of her pocket, praying mentally for a signal. Thankfully there was one, so she dialled 999.

"Which service do you require?"

"*All* of them," Kirsty stammered incredulously. "I'm stuck in the cellar of the bloody Spar and there are *vampires* outside!"

* * *

"Oh, good," Harold muttered. Raising his voice, he called for the others. "You need to hear this, guys!"

Emily and Abbie, as well as broad-shouldered, dark-haired 'gentle giant' Carter Guinness, jogged over to the control desk. The four of them made up the Blade Runners' base team and were the only ones who hadn't yet gone home.

"What's up?" Carter asked.

"Just intercepted a call," Harold replied. "Hope you haven't made any plans for tonight, 'cos we've got vampires."

Chapter 4

"Eat my *dust*, Pops," Sophie cackled, as Yoshi sped into first place on the Mario Kart course she, Edward and their father David were racing on. "I am the greatest!"

"Just my luck to end up as a Shy Guy," David growled. Stricken by a bomb, his grey Shy Guy spun wildly and tumbled into the Yoshi Falls waterfall.

"It's not luck," Edward reminded him, manoeuvring his own green Shy Guy into third. "Whoever doesn't have the game in their DS is always Shy Guy."

"Perfect," David sighed, now in twelfth place. "Next time I bagsy the game and Princess Peach."

"Why Princess Peach?" Sarah spluttered incredulously.

"She's the most agile. And the only pretty one."

Edward almost lost third place due to a burst of laughter. "Is it wrong to fancy a cartoon character?" he pondered through his chuckles.

David was too busy trying to reach eleventh place to respond. "I need a Torpedo Bob," he muttered.

"Bullet Bill," Edward corrected automatically, before noticing his Nokia was vibrating. As soon as he'd swept past Sophie and finished the race, Edward grabbed the mobile and looked at the screen.

INCOMING CALL, it read. UNKNOWN NUMBER.

He answered it, holding it up to his ear. "Hello?"

"*Is that Edward?*" said a girl's voice, a vaguely familiar one.

Edward frowned. "Yes... Who is this?"

"*Er, it's Daisy.*"

"Who?"

"*Daisy Grant. You know - in your form...*"

Edward was startled. Daisy Grant was a quiet fifteen-year-old, a Year 11 in his form. At St. Jude's, form groups were 'vertical' - each form contained four or five members of each year group. This was meant to integrate members of different year groups together, and though it seemed to have worked alright, Edward had never been particularly sociable (his only real friend from the group, Greg Wheeler, had died during the Gorakdezor incursion) and as he recalled, neither had Daisy.

"Daisy? How did you get my number?"

"*Listen, there's someth-*" she began anxiously, but then the line died.

"Well, that was plain weird," Edward declared. "This girl from my form has somehow got hold of my phone number."

"She probably fancies you," Sophie giggled.

"Silence, ten-year-old." He was about to press 'redial', when his mobile got another incoming call - this time from Harold Vandaleur. He thumbed the answer button.

"What's up?"

"*Oh, it's a biggie,*" Harold told him, laughing mirthlessly. "*We're heading to your village right now - well, Carter and Abbie are, and the others'll be on their way as soon as I've rung 'em. Good job you aren't too far from the action."*

"Lucky me."

* * *

"*Vampires*," Abbie shuddered, as she clambered out of the SUV passenger seat in full biker gear. "I can't *stand* bloody vampires."

"Understandable," her similarly leather-clad companion, Carter Guinness, pointed out as he headed over to the boot to unpack their weapons. "They are kind of meant to be sort of killer monsters from the darkest nightmares of the human race."

"Oh thanks, that really helps," she replied sarcastically, going over to join him. Together they unloaded the weaponry: two modified grenade launchers, now capable of firing any kind of large object; 'ammunition belts' of garlic cloves, for firing from the launchers; two stakes each; Glock semi-automatic pistols; and, just for old times' sake, Gorakdezor laser handguns.

"Sweet," Carter whistled, casting an eye over the assembled weapons.

They started walking briskly through the streets of Pinchbeck, eyes peeled for anything unusual. There was nothing visible, but a chill was in the air and there was a sense of foreboding - as if there was a predator lurking nearby, just about to pounce.

"When I was five or six, Mum and Dad went for a night out," Abbie whispered, though she wasn't sure why she was whispering. "They left my big brother to look after me and Lily, but he put on this really gory vampire film. Lily wasn't scared, but I had nightmares every night for weeks." She shivered. "I still don't like watching anything with vampires in it, let alone going up against the real thing."

"Ah well," Carter said reassuringly. "Nothing like killing one of your nightmares to stop you being scared of it."

Abbie still looked unsure. "S'pose..."

Soon the Spar came into view. The lights were still on, the door wide open, and there appeared to be no signs of trouble, but Carter and Abbie were wary of a trap. They entered the building cautiously, garlic guns at the ready.

"Way too quiet," Carter noted almost inaudibly, as they reached a fork in the maze of Spar aisles.

"Split up?" Abbie suggested, and Carter nodded before moving off down one aisle. Garlic gun outstretched before her, Abbie stepped into another - and almost tripped over a body.

Carter heard Abbie's squeal of shock, and turned and ran without hesitation back along his aisle and into hers. He found her standing over the dead body of a teenage girl.

"Sorry, I just panicked..." Abbie stammered, looking white as a sheet. Carter held up a hand to silence her.

"It's OK," he whispered gently, before kneeling to examine the victim. She was about seventeen or eighteen, very thin, and had striking black hair. Her skin was a ghostly pale colour, like her life had been sucked out of her, and there were two fang marks on her neck, so it was likely the life *had* been sucked out of her.

"Vampire kill," Carter said sadly. "The killer must have been pretty starving; poor girl's completely drained of blood."

"So is this her?" Abbie wondered. "The girl who called the emergency services?"

"Can't be sure; we need to check the rest of the store."

Abbie glanced over her shoulder, and caught sight of the ajar cellar door.

"Cover my back," she told Carter, heading off in the direction of the door. Seeing where she was going, Carter followed, and they approached with guns raised.

Nudging the door open with her foot, Abbie began to step cautiously down the stone staircase. She could hear Carter trying to breathe quietly behind her, as he kept his Glock at the ready.

The cellar was cold, a cold that chilled Abbie right to the core. Something evil was here, she could sense it, and from the almost inaudible shivering sound Carter was making, he sensed it too.

"Hello?" said a small voice in the darkness in front of them.

Abbie nearly opened fire there and then, the shock was so great. Carter remained slightly more composed and called out, "Who's there?"

"Please," the voice begged, and it was the obviously terrified voice of a teenage girl. "Help me, there are vampires everywhere..."

"It's alright," Abbie told her, trying to sound reassuring. "We're the good guys. I'm Queen Two, but you can call me QT. This is King Two - KT. You can trust us."

A figure moved in the darkness, and the two Blade Runners heard footsteps.

"Who *are* you?" the girl said, voice shaking as much as the rest of her as she approached them. "Wh-why are you dressed like bikers? Oh God, you've got guns..."

"We're the vampire rapid response team," Carter joked. Abbie rolled her eyes behind her visor.

"I think the more important thing here is: who are *you*? And what happened here?"

"I-I'm Kirsty," the girl stammered. "There were vampires... They got my friends..."

"How many vampires were there?" Carter asked.

"Loads... At least six... They ch-chased me down here, but then they said they'd l-leave me for later and they went back upstairs..."

Abbie was confused. "But they aren't upstairs - we checked the whole place. No vampires."

Kirsty looked terrified. "Th-then where the hell are they?"

And then the shadows that filled the room twisted and solidified into two huge vampires, who immediately pounced.

Chapter 5

"Get back!" Carter shouted, whirling and opening fire with his Glock. But he was too slow, and the vampires seemed to dissolve into black smoke, pale flesh turning dark and intangible as they rocketed forwards, and the bullets simply flew straight through the smoke and ricocheted off the wall behind it.

Abbie dived to the floor, tackling a screaming Kirsty down with her, and tried desperately to aim her Glock. The smoke had manifested back into two solid forms: one, a hulking grey-haired brute, had pinned Carter's arms behind his back, his own gun lying discarded on the floor as the other, a tall, lean vampire with a shock of white-blond hair, moved in for the kill. Firing wildly with everything else in her gun, Abbie sadly managed to miss the blond vampire completely.

"Time for a light bite," he cackled, baring his fangs. As Abbie watched, impotent, from the floor, with no time to reach any of her other weapons, the vampire lunged forwards to sink his fangs into Carter's neck.

There was a sudden blaze of light, and the blond vampire vanished. Eyes stung by the beam, Abbie blinked, a single tear dripping onto the stone floor. Carter winced at the brightness, but the large vampire holding him fared worse: screaming, he relinquished his grip on Carter and staggered backwards, clutching his face. Grey smoke, the kind that went with fire, escaped from beneath his palms as he moaned.

A helmeted, leather-clad figure stood at the top of the staircase, holding a very obvious gun.

"What, did I set it too high?" the figure said in Edward Blades' voice. "Just, he looked pretty pale, like he needed a sun tan..."

"You're bloody late, Venom!" Carter roared.

Stepping out of the gloom and descending the stairs, Edward made a 'whatever' W-sign with his gloved fingers, letting the gun dangle from a strap attached around his shoulder. "Better late than never, KT. Better late than never."

The huge vampire hissed with pain and fury, before morphing back into black smoke and whirling back into the shadows.

Abbie scrambled to her feet. "Weren't you going to try and stop him?"

Edward sniffed dismissively. "He obviously didn't fancy his chances, and I've got no appetite for killing any more than I have to." As he said this, he used his foot to sweep aside a newly-formed pile of dust on the floor - all that remained of the blond vampire, Abbie realised.

"And who have we here?" Edward continued, moving over towards Kirsty, who was huddled into a protective ball on the floor, petrified with fear. "Friend or foe?"

"Friend," Abbie assured him. "This is Kirsty, the girl who phoned for help."

"Kirsty," Edward said thoughtfully. "Cool name. Never known anyone called Kirsty though. Obviously I do now." He knelt down next to Kirsty, putting a reassuring gloved hand on her shoulder. "Hello, Kirsty. My name's Venom."

Kirsty managed a faint smile. "That's a weird name."

"Hey, it's not my real name. My real name isn't as cool. It isn't even as cool as yours."

"I've always hated my name," Kirsty confessed, then caught herself. "Hang on, who are you people anyway? The other guy said you were vampire response guys or something, but that can't be real, can it? And why are you dressed like bikers?"

"He was joking," Abbie told her. "We're not the vampire rapid response unit - not exactly, anyway."

"We deal with anything paranormal, not just vampires," Edward continued. "We wear biker gear to protect our identities, because if the authorities found out who we really are, they'd probably try and shut us down."

"So..." Kirsty said hesitantly, obviously scared of the question she was about to ask, "what do you mean by... paranormal?"

"Mostly, aliens. We get the odd other thing - ghosts for instance, which usually turn out to just be memories given projective form - but usually it's extraterrestrial life we deal with. This is the first vampire problem we've had, but we knew they existed - that's why we have these things." He held up the large gun he had shot the blond vampire with. "Light cannon. Shoots pure light energy - perfect for zapping vampires. Shame I had to use it, really - it only fires once and we've only got a handful of these babies. No idea how to recharge them, either."

She stared at him with eyes the deep brown colour of chocolate, not daring to let herself believe what she was being told. "You hunt... aliens?"

"We hunt aliens," Edward confirmed, and Abbie could almost hear the gleeful smile he was probably wearing. "Oh, and vampires - for one night only. Provided those were the only two of 'em."

Kirsty shook her head, eyes wide with horror. "No, it's not just two - there were loads of them! They could have spread halfway round the village by now!"

"Two were hard enough to handle," Carter said grimly. "If there are more, we could be about to find ourselves in the middle of a bloodbath."

"All right," Edward said with a sigh, "we need to find out how widespread this is. KT, take Kirsty back to base - only safe place for her if there really is a vampire invasion. Then get King One to call the others - everyone needs to get to Pinchbeck pronto, and I mean *everyone*. QT, you come with me - we're going on a whirlwind tour of Pinchbeck, no fee required."

Chapter 6

"Is it always this... *quiet*?" Abbie asked, shivering at the unusual cold. "It's bloody creepy."

"Welcome to Pinchbeck," Edward replied. "Mind you, it is quieter than usual. Here's hoping it's because everyone's just having an early night, rather than because everyone's been got by vampires."

"Did you *have* to say that?" Abbie moaned.

They were walking quickly and quietly along Pinchbeck's only A road, looking around constantly for anything out of place. Abbie had suggested, and Edward had agreed, that they change back into civilian clothing so they were less conspicuous. This meant that, dressed in t-shirts and jeans, they couldn't easily carry a shedload of weaponry around, so they had to make do with Gorakdezor laser guns (which looked a lot like toys anyway), stakes tucked into their belts, handguns in the back pockets of their jeans and a small metal device that Edward referred to as a 'surprise', which he kept in his pocket. They also wore mirrored sunglasses - as Edward had pointed out, vampires possessed hypnotic powers, so they needed to be able to reflect the hypnotic energy from vampire eyes.

"So, what were you up to when Harold rang you?" Abbie asked, trying to distract herself from the possible threat.

"Sister's birthday. We were at the Red Lion, planning to have a family meal. I was going to have a steak. Medium rare, nice and bloody..." His eyes glazed as he imagined the lost meal.

Abbie grimaced. "You're starting to sound like a vampire yourself."

He chuckled. "I was actually researching them in Ludgrove's database only the other day. Apparently they don't just come from Transylvania, but there are colonies all over Europe. Most of them have turned vegan since Alexei III took over as the vampire king, but there are the odd few who still have a taste for blood." Edward looked grim once more at this. "Including the ones we just fought, apparently."

The distraction tactic evidently hadn't worked. Resigning herself to the inescapable fact that the only topic they could discuss right now was vampires, Abbie asked, "So, where do you think tonight's lot came from?"

"God only knows. There are meant to still be carnivore vampires out there somewhere, but no-one's sure where exactly. Ludgrove's database has some of his theories on it though. There have been rumours of small carnivore colonies in Siberia, in Portugal, in Turkey... There's even news of a supposed group of renegades in Transylvania itself, planning to overthrow the vegan king and bring back the old ways of blood and dark rituals."

"Wonderful."

By now they had reached the edge of Clement Drive, the road linking the main road with St. Francis Avenue, the road Edward's family lived on. The first house they saw was obviously the right place to begin their search - the door was wide open, there was no sign of lights or indeed life, and one of the upstairs windows had been shattered.

Gesturing in the direction of the house and muttering 'Come on', Edward led Abbie down the path to the ajar door. Gorakdezor guns raised, they entered the house cautiously.

There had obviously been a disturbance: the living room had been completely trashed. The cushions of a sofa had been flung aside; the TV was lying on its front, surrounded by shards of its own screen; the coffee table had collapsed, presumably from some great impact; and the mantelpiece had been torn from the wall, scattering smashed ornaments and photographs with broken frames everywhere.

"I'm inclined to bet everything I have that this wasn't a domestic dispute," Edward said quietly.

"Because that would just be too easy," Abbie agreed, moving to the door at the other side of the room.

Before she could was even within reach of the door, black smoke poured out from under the door.

"Get back!" Edward shouted, charging forwards and raising his gun.

But the smoke had already solidified into a snarling vampire - *a girl*, Abbie just had time to think - and it threw itself on her, tackling her to the floor and pinning her down. The vampire girl hissed triumphantly, baring its fangs.

"Don't even think about it," Edward snarled, pressing his gun against the vampire's temple. "Get up, slowly, right now, or I'll fry you."

Reluctantly, the vampire hauled herself off Abbie, getting to her feet. With her hands behind her head, she faced Edward.

Edward gasped. "Rose!"

Still lying on the floor, Abbie glanced up at the vampire, taking in her appearance for the first time. She was about the same height as Edward, though less physically imposing, and had long, bright scarlet hair and a pretty, though pale, face. Her eyes blazed red, just as the eyes of the vampires in the Spar had, and her pupils had dilated to the point where they were just black lines, bisecting the crimson iris.

"Do you two *know* each other?" Abbie asked incredulously.

Hissing with outrage, the vampire girl started to back away from them - but Edward moved fast, throwing the 'surprise' device to the floor, between her feet. The device bleeped briefly, and then bars of ultraviolet light appeared as if from nowhere, surrounding the vampire girl.

"Try getting out of that without getting fried," Edward told the girl triumphantly. "And it also generates an energy field to prevent matter alteration, so don't try turning into smoke either."

The girl's face contorted with rage. "Let me *out* of here!"

"Don't you remember me, Rose?" Edward asked, looking dismayed. "It has been nearly four years, but we have talked on Facebook a lot; that's how I knew it was you..."

The girl Edward had called 'Rose' laughed cruelly, a dismissive sneer on her face. "Of course I remember you, Edward. I just don't care, that's all." But there was a hint of curiosity in her eyes as she added, "Mind you, pretty impressive tech. I had no idea slayers were this advanced."

"I'm no slayer," he assured her. "I'm just interested in anything paranormal."

Rose sniggered. "You don't change, *Doctor Who* boy."

"You were just as into *Doctor Who* as I was!" he protested, before catching a look from Abbie. "Anyway," he continued, "getting back to the matter in hand, back when I was in Kent you never mentioned you were a vampire..."

"I wasn't," she snapped back. "I got bitten about six days ago."

"And you decided to come up to Lincolnshire? Why?"

But Rose remained stubbornly silent.

Edward sighed and turned to Abbie. "Right, get me a clove of garlic."

Rose looked alarmed, but tried to hide it with another sneer. "You think you can just torture me into telling you everything? Well, I'll be happy to disappoint you, *old friend*." She almost spat the last two words, directing the full force of her anger at Edward.

Grimly, he took the garlic from Abbie and held it out in front of him. Stepping through the ultraviolet light and into the cage, he moved his hand - still holding the garlic - towards Rose's face. With no more room to back away, aware of the UV bars close behind her, Rose tried to stand her ground - but the garlic was less than an inch from her face when she cried out, "Stop!"

Edward lowered the garlic and stepped out of the cage. "So start talking."

Reluctantly, Rose started to tell them everything. She needed 'encouragement' from a garlic-wielding Edward, but eventually he and Abbie had everything they needed to know.

Rose was a friend of Edward's from almost five years earlier, when he and his family had lived in Kent. Six nights ago, Rose had been heading back from seeing her boyfriend James when she had been attacked by two vampires - one huge with grey hair, and the other tall and muscular with spiked white-blond hair. Edward recognised the two from her description as the attackers from the Spar. She had been dragged into an empty garden and shoved into the shed, where the grey-haired hulk - whose name was Marlowe - held her while the blond - 'Sickle' - drank some of her blood. She had struggled desperately, but felt herself weakening as Sickle drank more and more. Then they had dumped her on the floor of the shed and left her, helpless.

"Then I felt so much darkness - so many terrible thoughts - enter my mind," Rose continued. "It filled my senses, overcame my whole body - and it was *good*. So good. When I woke up, I was... different. Stronger. I felt I could do anything, be unstoppable... The dark thoughts that filled my head, that *still* fill my head..." She smiled savagely at this. "They felt *right*. I followed Sickle, and joined with him... and since then I have served him loyally, and fought at his command."

"So bitten vampires are brainwashed to be loyal to those who bite them," Edward said slowly. "Thought that was just a myth, but I guess not." He gestured for her to carry on.

Rose explained what Sickle had told her: that he was a carnivore vampire from Germany who, along with his friend Marlowe, was recruited by a vampire force from Siberia, who were travelling west with the intention of building an army. Their leader, Viktor Korbachev, was a Russian vampire and close friend of the last vampire king, Alexei II, a great supporter of drinking human blood. After Alexei II died, his son Alexei III took over and changed the vampire ways to vegetarianism, supplying the rest of vampirekind with 'soya blood' substitute. Korbachev wasn't happy with this, so he set up resistance groups of carnivorous vampires in east Romania and in his homeland of Siberia. Now he was leading his group west, to Britain, hoping to strike fast and take the British populace by surprise, and turn the whole country into a massive vampire stronghold within a few weeks.

"Korbachev wanted loads of fledglings - bitten vampires, like me - to act as foot soldiers in his army." Rose was fidgeting as she continued to talk, evidently bored with storytelling. "That's why Sickle got me, and that's why we're attacking Pinchbeck tonight. Every night for the next few weeks, we're attacking a village and turning all the breathers there into vampires. By the end of the month we should have an army powerful enough to overthrow the rest of the country."

"And you think people won't notice?" Abbie said disbelievingly. "That whole villages are losing all their inhabitants in one go?"

"Oh, they'll probably notice," Rose said, sniffing dismissively. "But they won't suspect *vampires* for a minute. Breathers are too stupid and narrow-minded."

"You say that, but you've just been outwitted by two," Edward told her.

"Like I matter. All that matters is that Korbachev and his army take over this country and then overthrow Alexei."

Edward tutted. "Still loyal? Sickle's dead, you know - I killed him. You don't have to follow Korbachev's orders any more."

Rose smiled evilly, and there was no hint of the person Edward had once known in her face. "You don't get it, do you? Sickle's opened my mind to the joy of blood, and fire, and death. I will serve Korbachev forever."

"Then I can't let you go," Edward replied sadly. He turned to Abbie. "Now we know the size of the threat, we need to get ready - the others should be on their way, so I need to meet up with them and round up the villagers. We'll get them all to the Red Lion; that's the easiest place to defend. You stay here and guard Rose - if we're making this a war, we're going to need hostages."

He strode out of the room, not sparing either Abbie or Rose another glance.

Great, Abbie thought unhappily. *Just me and the sucker, then.*

Chapter 7

Two jet-black SUVs pulled into the driveway outside the Red Lion pub. To the bafflement of onlookers, thirteen people - all dressed in biker gear - piled out of the vehicles, each one armed to the teeth with stakes, cannons and garlic ammo, Glocks and H&K sub-machine guns.

"Alpha team, secure the perimeter and take up defensive positions," Cathy ordered. In Edward's absence, authority deferred either to her or to Abbie's twin sister, Lily. "Beta, get every civilian sitting outside the Red Lion into the building. Control, come with me - we're holding a council of war in the bar."

"Yes, Asp," the other Blade Runners chorused dutifully, and moved out to complete their tasks. Robbie, George, Beth and Amy took up defensive positions surrounding the pub, facing outwards and preparing for any possible threat. The Beta team started rounding up people sitting outside and trying to persuade them to go inside.

Cathy, Carter and Emily approached the front door of the pub, but before they could reach it they were halted by a familiar commanding voice.

"I'll take it from here, Asp," Edward called from behind them.

Cathy sighed and turned to face Edward, who was now back in biker gear. "Better late than never, I suppose."

Edward ignored the jibe, instead quickly doing a head count of the Blade Runners present. "Where's King One?"

"Back at base, analysing the Mekrashi Sun Force Globe," Carter told him.

"I said I needed everyone here," Edward protested.

"Oh, so you wanted a civilian wandering around our base by herself then?" Emily said pointedly.

Remembering Kirsty, Edward conceded the point and without another word, he took the lead and the four of them entered the Red Lion.

***

The inside of the pub was in a state of confusion. People were milling around, unable to understand why there were bikers rounding people up. The TV was still showing BBC News 24 and their report on the Blade Runners, so some pubgoers had started to join up the dots. To make life even more fun for the teen vigilantes, a pair of policemen had stopped by for a soft drink each to break the monotony of patrol, and as Edward, Cathy, Carter and Emily walked in, both officers immediately deduced the identities of the 'bikers'.

"Hey," one of them shouted, moving forwards. "You're under arrest for vigilante action and causing a disturbance in a public place."

"Shut up and listen, PC Plod," Carter growled, stepping towards the officer. Although only seventeen, Carter had the kind of imposing physique people would cross the road to avoid, and the skinny forty-year-old constable was almost immediately quaking in his boots.

"We need to seal off this area," Edward said quickly, stepping smartly in between Carter and the policeman. "There is a hostile force in this village, and civilian lives are at risk."

The skinny constable rallied. "*You're* bloody civilians yourselves, and you're trying to make us police look bad! You're all nicked, the lot of you!"

"Listen, we need to work together!" Edward snapped back. "Your job is to protect innocent people; well, that's what we're trying to do."

The other officer, a middle-aged Indian man, stepped forwards. "What kind of hostile force?" he asked, a concerned expression cutting the permanent frown lines on his forehead even deeper.

"Vampires," Edward answered.

There was uproar. People were yelling at the four Blade Runners, shouting at them to *piss off, you load of loonies,* or variants of that theme. One man, a fat bald guy, even threw a punch at Emily. She intercepted it easily with one hand, and then shoved him aside with the other. Carter then stepped in between the two before a proper fight could get started.

"I'm going to have to call backup," the Indian officer told his skinny partner. "I can't let these people carry on causing this disturbance, but we can't arrest them all ourselves."

"We're serious," Edward told the policemen urgently. "Vampires are killing people in this village; at least two people have already died, and there are several more unaccounted for. Look, check the Spar - the place is abandoned, there's obvious signs of a disturbance, and the body of an eighteen-year-old girl is lying on the shop floor."

"That's not funny," the skinny PC snarled. "This has gone on long enough; why don't you just stop this stupid joke?"

Before Edward could open his mouth to argue again that they weren't joking, the customers in the restaurant area wandered into the bar to find out what was going on - including Edward's family.

Emily spotted them and groaned. "Oh *great*. As if things weren't complicated enough already."

Edward spoke quietly and urgently to the Indian officer. "We're just trying to help people; you have to trust us. If you don't, a lot of innocent people are going to die - or worse." Without waiting for the policeman to answer, he turned back to the other three Blade Runners. "Asp and KT, go and get the others together; I'll meet you back at the Land Rovers. QT, come with me."

As Cathy and Carter headed back outside, Edward and Emily pushed through the crowd of people, ignoring the protests and angry insults thrown at them. They came to a halt in front of Edward's parents and sisters. Emma stepped forward to confront him.

"What are you people playing at, coming in and babbling about vampires and stuff?" she said angrily. "You should all be locked up. This is beyond a joke!"

Sophie disentangled herself from her mother's protective arms and joined her elder sister. "Yeah!" she shouted at the two Blade Runners. "And you're ruining my sister's birthday!" Emma spared her a quick smile - though they had had their differences and constantly argued, she was grateful for her little sister's support when it mattered.

Pity they had to be a united front at precisely the wrong moment for me, Edward contemplated. He gave Emily a glance, and though they could not make eye contact through their blacked-out visors, Emily immediately understood what the look meant and shook her head vigorously.

"Don't do it," she cried desperately, but she couldn't stop Edward as he lifted his gloved hands and removed his helmet.

The other members of the Blades family blinked in amazement. What they were seeing could not be real.

Edward's mother, Sarah, was the first to find her voice. "Edward, what the *hell* are you playing at?"

"You're one of these Blade Runners," Emma stammered in shock. "Edward... You're one of these loonies..."

"Less of the 'loonies', thanks," Emily put in, removing her own helmet. Her long blonde hair unravelled over her leather-clad shoulders.

Edward's father David frowned. "Aren't you Emily Buzzer? The one who always forgets to bring a calculator to her exams?"

"Listen," Edward interrupted. "I know this is a shock, but we need to get on with things. I knew the only way I could get these people to trust me is if I reveal myself to you..."

"Edward Gideon Blades, stop this nonsense *right* now," Sarah shouted, her voice loud enough to stun the rest of the pubgoers into silence. "This has gone far enough - you can't go gallivanting around with these Blade Runners people; you're breaking the law!"

"We aren't breaking any laws, we're trying to protect people..." Emily tried, but Sarah wasn't having it.

"And you can be quiet, too! You can't just go around being 'above the law', Edward; the way I brought you up, I thought you understood that! You have to obey the law like everyone else - vigilante justice doesn't work, and it's illegal! Oh, I've heard all about these 'Blade Runners' on the news, running around pretending to protect people, but the truth is you are only making problems *worse*. Dealing with crime and the like is down to the police..."

"Oh, and where were *they* when our school was attacked by *aliens*?" Edward roared, finally drowning out his mother. "Yeah, you heard me: *aliens*. We never told the truth about what happened that day; about what happened to Greg and Lizzie and Amelia and Neil and Joanne and all the rest, because we knew you'd *never* believe us!"

He stopped abruptly, aware that everyone was watching him and his mother. Satisfied he had the attention of the entire Red Lion, Edward took a deep breath and continued, more calmly.

"Last October, our school was attacked by a race of aliens called the Gorakdezors. They froze time, so that we were stuck in the school at one precise moment - just us, a bunch of Year 12s against a swarm of predators and a group of dying aliens who wanted our bodies for themselves. No-one else could help - we were twenty-odd teenagers stranded by ourselves, and we had to fight back *ourselves*. It was up to *us*. And we did it - we wiped out those aliens before they got all of us. We might have been too late to save some people, but the majority of us got out unscathed - and even better, we saved the entire planet in the process!"

"Edward set up the Blade Runners to make sure no more aliens or any other kind of paranormal threat would cause any more lives to be lost," Emily added gently. "We've been going for six months and not a single one of us has been harmed in that time - and almost all the innocent people under threat from paranormal activity have survived because of us."

"Whereas if it were left to PC Plod, more would have died for certain," Edward concluded. "We're better equipped and better prepared for supernatural dangers than the police, and we've more experience in dealing with them as well. So please, let us do our job and save everyone in this village."

* * *

"What is taking Edward so long?" Nick wondered, anxiously drumming his hands on the side of one of the SUVs.

The Blade Runners were waiting in the Red Lion car park. The Alpha team were remaining in their defensive positions, while Cathy, Lily, Sky and Nick stood by the SUVs, inside which the others sat. There was no-one else outside the pub - they had convinced all the civilians to go inside by now.

Finally Edward and Emily stepped out of the pub's front door, and the Blade Runners were surprised to see their helmets off. Traipsing behind them were the two policemen, both of whom looked rather subdued.

"Well?" Sky asked as Edward and Emily approached.

"They didn't like it," Edward said wearily, "and I had to blow our cover to pretty much everyone in the pub, including my family, but we got them onside in the end. We need to divide and conquer - split into small groups and scout around Pinchbeck; round up civilians and get them back here. Lily and Nick, go to Number 1 Clement Drive - Abbie's holding a vampire prisoner there and she'll need back-up - but whatever happens, the prisoner stays *alive*. I'm staying here to prepare the Red Lion - we're going to get ready for a siege."

Chapter 8

"I'm not sure this is such a good idea," Luke said anxiously as he followed Bob up the drive to 37 Parker Street.

"Only idea I've got right now," Bob replied.

"We could be trying to round up civilians, like Edward told us to!"

"Or we could find something that'll tip the balance of power in our favour," Bob said pointedly. "Come on, Ed beat the Gorakdezors by turning their own technology against them - sabotaging the devices they used to control their big green pets. If we try to fight the vampires with their own kind..."

"We'll get killed," Luke insisted.

Bob sighed. "Have a little faith, Tucker."

The house they were approaching was a bungalow with blacked-out windows. The garden was wild and overgrown, and the paint on the front door was peeling. Clearly the residents didn't take much care of the place.

Bob raised a clenched fist and thumped hard on the door. "Open up, Rossy!"

There was no answer.

"We don't have time for this," Bob muttered, and delivered a powerful roundhouse kick that would have the average grown man clutching his chest and choking helplessly on the ground. The door broke clean off its hinges and fell to the floor inside the house.

Bob gave Luke a brief grin, before stepping over the door and into the house. After a moment's hesitation, Luke followed him.

Inside, in contrast with the deteriorating exterior, the house was pretty normal; the boys found themselves in a sitting room with a three-seat sofa, a flatscreen TV, a coffee table and a mantelpiece. Luke frowned.

"Are you sure we've got the right house?" he wondered.

"You have," came a hoarse whisper from behind them.

Luke and Bob nearly jumped out of their skin. Looking around frantically, they saw a dark figure standing in the doorway.

"Didn't expect to see you two again," the figure hissed.

Raising his gun, Luke took in the figure's appearance: it was a young man of average height and build, wearing a black shirt and grey jeans. He had angular features and a pale complexion, and his eyes were a dull red-brown. He noticed Luke's Glock and laughed slightly.

"You can put that away," he chuckled. "I'm a vegetarian, as well you know."

The young man pushed past Bob and sat down heavily on the sofa. "So, Undertuck, what can I do you for?"

"Rossy, mate," Bob said quickly, "we need your help. There are more vampires in Pinchbeck, and they aren't vegans."

Dave Ross raised one eyebrow. "You expect me to believe that?"

"People have already died," Luke put in, "and things are gonna get worse. We need someone on the inside, someone who knows vampires and can help us get to them..."

Rossy snorted. "Like I said, I'm veggie. I don't know what makes bloodsuckers tick; I haven't had a drop of real blood in my life."

"You're the only chance we have," Bob pleaded.

After a moment, Rossy sighed. "I guess I owe you both for not telling anyone about my little secret... Oh, all right then. My granddad's a sucker slayer, so I've picked up a thing or two from him."

He got to his feet. "So, what's the plan?"

***

The Red Lion was a hive of activity. Edward had organised everyone into building barricades and barriers throughout the pub - the entrances were blocked with tables and chairs, and there were walls made of table tops blocking paths at every turn.

The main bar area on the ground floor had become both the base of operations and the front line of defences. Emily, the Indian PC James Chandra, and a group of civilians - bruisers mostly, nearly all young men - were getting themselves battle-ready. Everyone else was packed into the upstairs restaurant, where Sarah Blades and the skinny policeman, Andy Scarlet, had taken charge. Every last man was armed with a weapon of some sort - even if it was just a tableleg, a chair or a kitchen knife.

Several people were placing booby traps and weapons throughout the building - the Red Lion had a few corridors and side rooms on each floor, and this, Edward had emphasised, was a good thing, as it allowed more opportunities for laying traps. Edward and his father could be found in the pub's attic, fixing a crossbow to the inside of a skylight - ready to fire down on vampire attackers.

"This reminds me of our old pub, back in Kent," Edward reminisced. Then, to his annoyance, he sneezed twice in quick succession. "The dust reminds me too..."

"So," David said heavily, "how did you get all this stuff?" At Edward's enquiring look, he indicated the crossbow. "Like this, and all the weapons you and your other 'Blade Runners' are showing off."

"Oh, Mr. Ludgrove gave them to us," Edward explained. Seeing David was even more confused by this, he continued. "Our old headmaster? The one who left last November? He resigned because he figured out that I knew he was an alien investigator. Before he went he gave me a key to this big warehouse, stuffed with weapons and alien tech - said it was all mine if I wanted it."

"A curse upon that man," David said wearily. "I'm sure it's a good teacher's responsibility to make sure his students *don't* get their hands on guns and things."

"Well, he had already resigned by that point; I guess the 'duty of care' rule didn't apply any more..."

"Edward, this is serious," David snapped. "You're putting yourself in danger - and your friends too. What if one of you got killed?"

"We live with that danger every day, and we've been so ready for it to happen that in six months, none of us have died," Edward said calmly.

"Yes, but maybe you've just been lucky," David protested desperately. "Please, Edward, I'm begging you - stop this absurd vigilante thing before you get yourself and your friends killed."

"That's assuming we make it through tonight," Edward reminded him. "But come on, let's face it - if I hadn't set up the Blade Runners, no-one would know that vampires even exist, let alone that they're planning to take over the country."

David couldn't argue with that, so he stomped off to find Emma. Edward paused for a moment, considering his father's point.

What if our luck is about to run out? he pondered. *The vampire threat is very powerful. Maybe tonight's the night my whole 'Blade Runners' project comes crashing around my ears.*

But if he kept wondering whether he was going to die tonight or not, he'd never get anything done, so Edward put his fears aside and headed back downstairs to marshal the troops.

***

Janine South was on her third glass of wine. She was waiting for her eldest daughter to return home, and was passing the time with wine and *Jeremy Kyle*. Truth be told, Janine was unbearably worried about her daughter. Ivy had left school after sixth form with no A-levels and immediately started wasting her life - partying, boozing and picking up random guys, some of whom seemed to be several years older.

There was a knock at the door.

"Let me in, Mum!" Ivy shouted through the letterbox.

Janine sighed, placing her glass on the coffee table and wandering through to the front door. After a moment's fumbling with the key, she got the door unlocked and pulled it open.

Ivy stood alone on the doorstep, her hair - which had started the night so immaculate - hanging limp, and her mascara smeared across her cheeks.

"And what time do you call this?" Janine said drily. "Oh, not dragged any random guys back here this time? Or have you just been with one and had your heart broken?"

"Have I always been a disappointment, Mum?" Ivy asked calmly.

Janine frowned, not expecting the question - or the way Ivy had asked it. "Er..."

"You're never happy to see me any more," her daughter continued. "You're always shouting at me, or complaining, or giving me icy glares... Where did we go so wrong?"

"I wish I knew," Janine replied, feeling a wave of sadness threatening to overcome her. "I don't know what I did wrong, but you didn't turn out the way I wanted you to... All these late nights, all the partying, all the blokes..."

"I can change though," Ivy said suddenly. "If I wasn't right, Mum, if I didn't turn out the way you hoped, I can change..." A sly look started to creep into her eyes. "I *have* changed."

Janine felt suddenly uneasy. "Where's Annabelle?"

"She's dead," Ivy replied, and smiled - a wide, wide grin that showed her teeth.

Including the huge fangs where her canines should have been.

"Ivy?" Janine spluttered, horrified.

"Let me show you what it's like, Mum," Ivy crooned. "Let me give you the power I've been given..."

And then her eyes blazed red.

***

"You look bored," Rose commented.

Abbie, sitting on the reassembled cushions of the sofa, glowered at her prisoner through her mirrored glasses.

Rose tutted. "Fine, don't talk to me then. Just thought it'd pass the time until one of your pals turns up and stakes me. Or until one of my pals turns up and drinks your blood."

"Shut up," Abbie snapped.

"At last, a reaction!"

Contrary to Rose's perceptive opinion, Abbie was not bored - she was on edge, half expecting a vampire to pounce at any given moment. She was mentally preparing herself for an ambush, and Rose's talk didn't help her concentration at all.

Then again, she considered, *that's probably why she's talking in the first place.*

Aloud she said, "You can keep trying to irritate me all you like; I'm not going to do anything. Edward gave me orders to keep you prisoner until another Blade Runner gets here, so that's what I'm going to do."

"Because you always do as Edward tells you."

Abbie gritted her teeth. "Yes, actually."

"I reckon you've got nice eyes," Rose said abruptly. "Wish I could see them; your face is pretty enough for you to have really lovely eyes."

Abbie was floored momentarily by the swerve in the topic. "Er, yeah, I guess," she stammered, flummoxed.

"What colour are they?" Rose continued eagerly.

"Sort of green-ish," Abbie replied awkwardly. "What's with the sudden eye obsession?"

The vampire shrugged. "Just curious. What d'you mean, green-*ish*? What shade of green are they?"

Abbie realised what she was trying to do, and bristled. "Look, you're not getting me to take my glasses off! I know vampires can hypnotise people, and I'm not falling for your tricks!"

"I wasn't," Rose said quickly, a look of pure innocence on her pale face. "I was just making conv-"

"I don't *want* to have a conversation with you!" Abbie shouted. "I'm your jailor, not your friend! Just shut up, or I'll probably stake you myself - you and any of your other pals who happen to show up here!"

Rose smirked. "Nah, you talk big. You're too scared to fight any of us..."

"I am *not* scared of you and your friends! Bring 'em on! All your vampire chums can come on in and fight me, '*cos I'm ready*!"

Then a massive impact hit Abbie squarely in the side, and she crumpled to the floor immediately.

A dark figure stood over her as she lay on her front, clutching her stomach and coughing violently. "You sure about that, girlie?" the figure said - the deep voice of a man, accented with Russian.

Abbie's glasses fell off as the Russian rolled her onto her back and pinned her down with his huge booted feet.

"I've used that punch for surprise attacks thousands of times, on victims far bigger than you," he laughed, kissing his knuckles triumphantly. "Never fails. Thanks for inviting me in, by the way."

Abbie tried to reach her Glock, which now lay discarded on the floor nearby, but the powerful Russian had her trapped. His eyes blazed a brilliant red - and as she glanced up at them, filled with fear, his stare fixed on her eyes.

The bright crimson fire within those glistening orbs seemed to pour out and into Abbie's own eyes, filling her mind. She found she could not look away - her gaze was locked with his, and as the seconds of helplessness ticked by, she felt that something was being drained out of her. Her mind? Her willpower? All Abbie knew was when she tried to look away, to reach for a weapon, to do *anything*, she just couldn't. A sudden calmness seemed to wash over her, and she relaxed. So what if she couldn't move? Maybe it wasn't such a terrible thing if she just stayed where she was, gazing into the Russian's scarlet eyes.

Abbie was smart enough to understand that she had been hypnotised, but she was also too hypnotised to care. The Russian finally looked away, knowing his victim's mind was already in a grip of iron, and disappeared from Abbie's unmoving line of vision - leaving her lying still and calm on the floor, staring up at the ceiling.

A few seconds later, the lilac glow from Rose's UV cage vanished. Abbie heard Rose's voice.

"Thank you so much, master," the recently converted vampire purred. "It means more than I can say that a glorious leader like you would personally free a worthless fledgling like me."

The Russian - who Abbie dimly realised must be Viktor Korbachev, leader of the vampire invaders - gave a short sharp bark of laughter. "Don't flatter yourself, eh, Rosie? You're right; I would never usually risk my un-life to save a freak of supernature like you. But every able-bodied vampire - born or bled - must be free and ready to subjugate the population of this oversized Atlantic rock, and in times of war a good general must enter the fray himself, to protect all his troops."

"Of course, master. And I beg your forgiveness for being captured by breathers," Rose grovelled. "It will not happen again, this I swear. You know I remain eternally loyal to you and to our cause, master..."

"Save the toadying for later, Rose, we have a village of breathers to feast upon," Korbachev interrupted. "My other soldiers are gathering near the local tavern, preparing to launch an attack on the mortals hiding out there. Go and join them, and tell them I will arrive shortly - and then the main meal shall be served." He moved back into Abbie's vision, and she saw that he wore a savage grin. "I just want my starter first..."

I'm about to die, Abbie thought slowly.

When subjected to vampire hypnosis, the mortal mind usually feels no emotion - it becomes calm; cold; analytical of its surroundings. But at this moment, some tiny part of Abigail Kilgour's mind stirred, straining against the shackles of Korbachev's control. An image floated to the surface of her senses, that miniscule free section of her consciousness fighting to make this image - that of her twin sister, Lily - the last thing she ever saw.

I'll never see Lily again.

And that thought filled Abbie's mind as Korbachev's fangs sank into her neck.

Chapter 9

Gravel crunched as the big black SUV pulled into the driveway.

"The South residence," Robbie announced, leaning forward in the driver's seat. "Or so Edward's list of neighbours tells me."

"Thank God we remembered he made one," Cathy added. "On a day off."

"What exactly is wrong with the guy, anyway?" George wondered. "Why would anyone want to write a list on their day off? Too much like hard work, as far as I'm concerned..."

Cathy glared at him. "He's autistic, George. Apparently autistic people tend to like listing stuff."

"Yeah, but usually his lists are pointless! 'List of Doctor Who episodes', 'List of Merlin characters', 'List of girlfriends Edward Blades has ever had'... Actually, I reckon he wouldn't bother with that one, since he's only had one. And she's glaring at me right now."

"Look, we need to get on with things," Robbie interrupted as Cathy opened her mouth to retaliate. "For all we know, half of Pinchbeck could have been wiped out while you two have been bickering." And with that, he grabbed his Glock and clambered out of the SUV.

"Touché," Cathy muttered, and she and George followed.

It was only a short walk from where the SUV was parked to the front door of the house, but the three teenagers were on edge and trying to be careful, prepared for an ambush at any moment, so it took twice as long for them to make the journey. As soon as they reached the front door they heard the sobbing coming from inside.

"Hello?" Cathy called.

"Shush," Robbie told her quietly but urgently. "Could be a trap."

"What if someone's hurt, or in danger?" Cathy pointed out.

"Oh, get out of the way," George muttered, and launched a powerful kick, knocking the door off its hinges.

There was a startled cry from within. Cathy looked, but all the lights were off and she could barely see through the gloom.

"Is there anyone there?" she called, stepping cautiously through the doorway and into the dark living room. "Please, we just want to help; you might not believe this but there are vampires..."

She fumbled on the nearby wall for a light switch, but she was saved the trouble when a lamp came to life at the other side of the room.

Cathy clutched a hand to her heart. "Jesus, you scared the life out of me there!"

A drawn figure was standing by the lamp. "Who are you?" the figure, a middle-aged woman with cropped fair hair, asked.

"We're here to help," Robbie assured her.

"I know about the vampires," the woman told them, her voice shaking. "My daughter, she..." She hesitated, tears rolling down her cheeks. "She's one of th-them..." And she broke down, sobbing uncontrollably.

Cathy moved instinctively to comfort her, putting her hands around the woman.

"I'm so sorry," she whispered soothingly. "But you're going to be okay now. What's your name?"

"J-Janine," the woman stammered.

"Okay, Janine, and what's your daughter's name?"

"Ivy..."

"Right, we're getting everyone together at the Red Lion, so we'll take you down there too; it should be safer there. Have you got anyone else; any other relatives? Janine?"

"My husband, he's at the pub already... My other three kids, they're all asleep..." Janine started sobbing again.

"Right, okay, Janine, listen. You and your kids are coming with us; we've got an SUV outside, and Robbie and George'll carry the kids out..."

"We will?" George said incredulously.

Cathy shot daggers at him over Janine's shaking shoulder.

"We will," he conceded, and followed Robbie through to the bedrooms.

***

"Let's get moving, people!" Sophie roared. "Positions!"

Final preparations for the siege were taking place, and small but loud Sophie had been recruited as a human megaphone, standing atop the bar and passing on orders from Edward to the civilians. At her command, everyone moved to the positions Edward had given them.

Edward, Emily, David and PC Chandra were in charge of the main force of defenders on the ground floor. These were some of the burliest young men in the village, including Alex Herald, a stocky lad of seventeen, who was reigning champion of the 'Strongest Youth' contest at the annual village carnival.

Anyone who didn't want to fight on the front line, primarily women and old people, were in the upstairs restaurant, with some other defenders dotted around in the upstairs corridors. The other four Blade Runners - Beth, Amy, Sky and Tasia - were in defensive positions outside the building.

As Sophie watched, the defenders half-settled in their positions, on edge and waiting for word of the vampires' arrival. She overheard Chandra mutter a comment to Edward as they passed the bar. "I wish I could've got through to my colleagues," he said. "They're not answering, I must've radioed about fifty times."

"They must be blocking the frequency," Edward replied. "They've taken down the phone lines as well, about ten minutes after the Spar attack apparently. On the bright side, no-one else is coming into danger."

"Yeah, but we've got no back-up," Chandra pointed out. "Apart from your lot. How come your radios are still working, anyway?"

"We're on a different frequency," Edward said, obviously choosing not to acknowledge Chandra's point about the lack of reinforcements. Neither of them spoke again.

As the minutes ticked by in silence, Sophie began to feel a little agitated - if the vampires were going to attack, why couldn't they just get on with it?

Suddenly Tasia's voice, half-shrouded in static, blared out of Edward's radio: "*Lyre to Venom. Savane and Keelback are coming up to the front of the pub with... someone I can't identify from inside a hedge.*"

Sophie giggled a little at this.

Edward snatched the radio and spoke rapidly into it. "Received and understood, Lyre." He stood, motioning to Clyde Gillen, the lean twenty-year-old landlord's son, to open the front door. Clyde shoved aside the heavy barricade, with a little help from Bernard South, and hauled the hefty door open.

Sure enough, Bob and Luke were standing in the pub's porch, along with someone Edward had not seen in almost two years.

"Rossy!" he gasped. "What the hell are *you* doing here?"

Rossy nodded in the direction of Bob and Luke. "Undertuck recruited me to help deal with your little vampire problem."

Bemused, Edward glared at Bob and Luke. "And why the hell did you two do that?"

Bob shuffled awkwardly. "Well... you see... the thing is..."

"I'm a vampire," Rossy interrupted.

There was, once again, immediate uproar. Everyone grabbed the nearest and most available weapon - Clyde dived for a plank of wood on the floor, while Sophie grabbed a wine bottle and held it by the neck like a club. Edward and Emily both went for their guns, training them on Rossy's chest.

"Wait!" Bob cried, stepping quickly into the path of his comrades' guns. "Let me explain..."

Emily snorted. "What, let you explain why you brought a vampire into our little fortress? Are you out of your tiny *minds*, Undertuck?"

"He's not like other vampires, he's a vegan," Luke interrupted.

"You expect us to believe that?" David snarled, raising a tableleg angrily.

Edward was thinking furiously, remembering the information about vampires from the Blade Runners' database. He remembered how the new vampire king was a vegan, how he had turned away from blood and murder and had most of vampirekind abstain from their carnivorous ways. *Is Rossy really a vegan, or is this just a ruse by Korbachev to get a man on the inside?*

"Start talking," he growled.

Looking even paler than usual, Rossy stammered, "I've never drank a drop of breather blood. I've been a vegan all my life, and so was my mum. She lived in Russia back in the old days of Alexei II, the last vampire king... My mum and a bunch of other Russians were about the only vegan vampires in the world.

"My dad was a vampire slayer - so's my granddad, actually. Dad went to Russia to kill off some of the king's lieutenants, and he found the vegan settlement. He met Mum, and she told him about how her little tribe refused to drink mortal blood, and he... Well, he let them live. He even set up camp in their village, while he worked out how to get at the carnivore lot.

"But before he could, one of the king's most fearsome carnivores, a Russian called Viktor Korbachev, attacked the camp. By himself, he killed every man, woman and child; every single vegan in that camp." At this, Rossy smiled sadly. "Except my mum. She got away with my dad, and they both came back to England. My granddad didn't trust Mum, but he let her stay. After Mum had me, Mum and Dad went off on a mission to slay a bunch of carnivorous vampires in London. Granddad promised to look after me for them until they got back." Rossy looked grim. "They never did."

"Luke found out who Rossy was a few weeks before he dropped out of school," Bob put in. "He told me, and we confronted him. He told us his story and we promised to keep it secret..."

"I had to leave," Rossy explained. "My sixteenth was coming up."

Alex Herald grunted. "What's that got to do with anything?"

"Before that age vampires are pretty much exactly like mortals," Luke explained. "On their sixteenth birthday they get all their powers and a fatal allergy to sunlight to boot, so Rossy couldn't keep coming to school."

"But... how can you be a *vegan* vampire?" Clyde protested. "I thought all vampires were bloodsucking creeps."

"Ta," Rossy replied, looking rather wounded.

"Most are vegans, actually," Edward told the group. "Mainly cos the current vampire king is. The last king died a few years back; he was big on blood hunts and dark rituals. There are barely any bloodsuckers left any more; it's just our bad luck that a lot of them are here, now."

"I've got as much reason to fight back against Korbachev as anyone," Rossy concluded. "I want to help. I haven't slain a carnivore vampire before, but I want to - sort of to get them back for my mum and dad."

David pulled Edward to one side and spoke urgently. "Do you really think we can trust this guy? He could be a Trojan horse."

Edward shrugged. "I don't know... All I know is Bob and Luke both trust him, so for the moment I'm going to."

He turned back to Rossy and the others. "All right, Rossy; you can stay. But I want Emily to stick to you like glue - you don't go anywhere without her. If this is a trick, Emily will be first to know, and then you're a dead vampire. If it isn't, then I'm sorry about this, but I need to take precautions - one big mistake on my part, and all of us could die tonight."

***

It had taken a while - and a lot of effort on Robbie and George's part - but all the Souths were now loaded into the SUV. The youngest two kids were still out for the count and snoring gently, but eleven-year-old Jessica stirred occasionally before resuming sleep. Cathy had persuaded Janine to get in the car as well, and the events of the last few hours combined with the alcohol she had drunk had finally overwhelmed her - she was spark out on the seat next to seven-year-old Ralph, his head resting on her arm.

Cathy watched the sleeping family from the passenger seat, a weary smile on her face.

"Mission accomplished," Robbie sighed, collapsing into the driver's seat.

"Thank God that was the last house," George put in, as he clambered into the back of the SUV. "Now everyone else is barricading themselves into their homes or they've gone to the Red Lion..."

"So now we can go there too," Cathy concluded, nodding. "Let's go."

Robbie got the car keys out of his pocket - and there was a huge crash, as some massive impact hit the side of the SUV.

The Souths all woke immediately, with screams of shock. Cathy jolted out of her seat so explosively she banged her head on the roof. Robbie dropped the keys in shock, while George swore loudly as he fell sideways off his seat.

There was a snarl of inhuman rage and bloodlust from outside.

"Mummy, what's going on?" Ralph wailed, hugging his mother tightly. Janine didn't reply - she was shaking with fear and confusion. Jessica and ten-year-old Philippa were screaming and clutching each other, panicked expressions on their faces.

"Bastard vampires hit us, guys!" George roared from the back of the SUV.

Robbie reached for his gun, glancing at the passenger seat to confirm Cathy had as well - but she was clutching her head and groaning. "Cathy, what's the matter?" he said urgently.

"Banged my bloody head," Cathy moaned.

"Great." Robbie glanced out of the window - and jumped at the sight of a huge man with tufts of grey hair.

"I'll get 'em, Robbie," George yelled. "You get the SUV fired up and ready for a quick getaway."

"On it," Robbie shouted back, reaching down and fumbling for the keys on the floor.

Ignoring the terrified cries of the Souths, George pulled a cannon and a bunch of garlic cloves to him, shoving the cloves into the ammo chamber. Then he shifted so the cannon was aimed at the back doors of the SUV, and launched a powerful kick, knocking the doors open.

There was an immediate roar of triumph from outside the vehicle - but the vampires' glee was short lived as George opened fire indiscriminately, blasting garlic out of the SUV doors in every direction. The creatures screamed as the garlic hit their flesh and burnt it away, causing a slow but inevitable and agonising death. The grey-haired vampire launched himself at the doors with a savage roar, only for a clove to hit him full in the face and send him reeling.

"Right, punch it, Robbie!" George bellowed, hooking his feet around the bottoms of the back doors and tugging them shut again. Mere moments later Robbie shoved the key into the ignition and the SUV roared into life. Robbie wasted no time and slammed his foot down, sending the vehicle and its passengers tearing across the gravel driveway and out onto the tarmac of the St. Francis Avenue road.

***

Viktor Korbachev knew he was an impressive being, even amongst vampires. Just to look at him was to be awestruck: at almost seven feet tall, the Russian was muscular with a handsome, defined face, and his smile could charm the wildest of animals into submission. Even without the use of his hypnotic skills, he had enough charisma to build an army of his own - which, of course, was exactly what he was doing.

He stood in front of at least a dozen vampires, Rose amongst them. All were kneeling before him, their expressions a mixture of devotion and bloodlust. Rose in particular looked eager to join her first major battle, excitement flashing in her eyes at the thought of all the human blood soon to be spilt. As Korbachev continued to watch his 'soldiers', more and more emerged from the darkness to join them at his feet. Korbachev noticed one vampire in particular, a blonde fledgling who he remembered pledging to bring more recruits to him, returning alone.

"You," he snarled, his guttural voice at odds with his appearance. "Where are the others you promised?"

Ivy looked ashamed. "They wouldn't come, my master. My mother wouldn't let me into the house."

Korbachev felt a surge of anger, but suppressed it. It wouldn't do to lose control now, not over such a trivial matter, and moments before a battle. He needed to keep a clear head.

"Never mind," he said slowly, now addressing the whole crowd. "There are plenty more where that came from. The humans have built a stronghold in the local inn - so this is where we shall strike next. All who resist shall be destroyed, but save a few to add to the army."

He turned and stalked off, expecting the other vampires to follow swiftly. Which they did, obviously.

"But, my lord," Rose began tremulously, evidently scared to be speaking out of turn. "How will we enter the building? No-one's going to invite us in; not now they know what we are..."

Korbachev sniggered. "Fledglings. The first rule you need to learn is this: you don't need an invitation if there's no more building."

***

The Red Lion was filled with deathly silence. Everyone was crouched behind upturned tables and hastily-built barricades, trying to breathe as quietly as possible. The situation was the same on both floors - it was as if they were at a surprise party, Sophie reflected from behind the downstairs bar, waiting for the recipient to walk in. Except when the vampires *did* arrive, they would find garlic as the only party food on the menu.

Sophie fidgeted with the club-like tableleg she had been armed with. "This is getting uncomfortable," she murmured softly. Crouching next to her, Alex Herald gave her a sympathetic smile.

And then the vampires arrived.

They walked out of the darkness surrounding the pub, moving into the glare of street lamps. Not even bothering to conceal themselves, they began to spread out, moving off in either direction to surround the building. Edward exchanged a look with PC Chandra as both of them half-lay next to the window, right at the front of the defences.

David stuck his head around a table, catching Edward's eye. "What are they playing at?" he mouthed. Edward shrugged as a response.

"Pincer movement," PC Chandra told him, almost inaudibly. "That's tactical."

Korbachev appeared in the midst of the small army. It was easy to tell that he was the leader - he had an aura of pure charisma, and the other vampires moved around him almost reverentially. One girl, who must have been fourteen or fifteen, was jostled slightly by another vampire, and accidentally fell onto Korbachev's foot. Moving with unbelievable speed, the tall Russian reached down and seized the young vampiress by the hair, hauling her to her feet. Then he raked his razor sharp fingernails - almost like talons - down her cheek, leaving horrific claw marks.

"This is sick," Chandra whispered, and Edward was inclined to agree with him.

"That's my daughter!" Bernard shouted suddenly, making everyone jump. "That's my daughter, look, she's in the middle of all of them!"

Edward looked frantically through the crowd, and almost immediately spotted Ivy South.

"Ivy!" Bernard yelled, leaping out from behind his table and running for the door. "*Ivy*!"

"Bernard, get back here!" Edward called after him desperately. "Don't go out there, it's too dangerous!"

But it was too late. Bernard smashed the defences aside and ran outside, faster than anyone had ever seen him run, heading straight for the vampires.

"Ivy, get away from them!" he bellowed. "It's not safe!"

Ivy just laughed cruelly.

Bernard skidded to a halt, confusion filling his face. Then this turned to fear, as he realised the dangerous position he was now in.

He turned tail and ran back in the direction of the pub - but he wasn't quite fast enough. Edward and the others could only watch, horrified, as six vampires launched themselves onto Bernard, literally tearing him limb from limb.

"Let battle commence," Chandra said quietly.

Chapter 10

"Which house did he say it was?" Lily called as she jumped out of the SUV and headed for the back doors.

"Number one," Nick replied, hauling the doors open as she approached. "Not particularly hard to remember."

Lily raised her eyebrows. "All right, keep your hair on. Have we got everything we need?"

"And then some." Nick pulled out two rapid fire garlic cannons, four iron stakes, and a couple of UV grenades. "Right, how about you go in and meet up with Abbie while I stay out here and keep an eye out for more vampires?"

After a beat, Lily nodded. "Ten four, Boa. I'm going in." With that, she marched up the driveway and through the open door of number one, Clement Drive.

The minutes ticked by. Nick leaned against the side of the SUV, growing steadily more anxious as there was still no sign of either sister, or their prisoner.

When ten minutes passed with still no word from the other two, Nick gave in and switched on his radio. "Boa to Viper, what's the situation in there? Over."

There was a crackle of static. Twenty seconds passed.

"Boa to Viper, please respond, I'm getting kind of worried out here. Over."

Crackle. Ten seconds.

"Lily? Abbie? Either of you, just pick up the damn radio. You've got ten seconds or I'm coming in there. Over."

Crackle.

Five seconds. He started walking.

The scene that greeted him inside the house was something out of a horror film. The living room carpet was soaked in blood. The air was filled with the tangy smell of sour metal. A sofa's cushions had been scattered, the TV was smashed, the coffee table was destroyed and ornaments and photographs were everywhere.

And kneeling in the middle of the nightmare was one twin, cradling the lifeless body of the other.

Nick reeled, feeling as though he had been punched in the stomach. It was as if the world had lurched, trying to cope with the scale of what had happened - because Abbie Kilgour could not be dead; it just wasn't possible. It was too devastating a scenario to even imagine, and yet the proof was there in front of him.

After a minute, or maybe a year, Nick found his voice. "Lily?" he croaked, still barely able to speak and yet expressing so much with that one word.

Lily spoke, and that was the most terrifying part. Because she didn't shout; she didn't cry; she didn't scream at the heavens, howling at the injustice of what had happened to her sister.

"I'm going to the pub," she announced, and she was absolutely calm.

***

At 12.30pm US time on November 22, 1963, President John Fitzgerald Kennedy of the United States of America was assassinated in Dealey Plaza, Dallas, Texas. He was travelling in a Presidential motorcade car with his wife Jacqueline, Texas Governor John Connally, and Connally's wife Nellie, when the gunman, Lee Harvey Oswald, stepped out of the crowd and opened fire, killing Kennedy and wounding Connally.

The moment was described as 'the shot heard around the world', as it was a moment that reportedly everyone alive remembers being able to describe, almost as if everyone in the world paused, feeling the loss of the 35th President of the USA. Other events in history have been described similarly: the phrase is also used to describe the moment when Austrian Archduke Franz Ferdinand and his wife Sophie were assassinated by Gavrilo Princip in Sarajevo, Bosnia-Herzegovina, on June 28, 1914, the action that caused events within global government to spiral out of control and to lead to the beginning of the First World War.

On 5 May, 2013, at 02.59am UK time, another such event occurred: 'the shot heard around Pinchbeck' was a moment that no-one who lived there, even those not caught in the midst of it, would ever be likely to forget.

It was the moment a barrage of fireballs hit the side of the Red Lion pub and tore it open like a packet of crisps.

The blast was phenomenally powerful: every single one of Korbachev's army had used their pyrokinetic abilities at once, and the result was spectacular. The side of the building was devastated to the point where the wall just crumbled and fell away, exposing the building's insides. The impact of the blast shook the whole pub, smashing windows on both floors and spraying inhabitants with shards of glass.

Vampires whooped and bellowed with glee as they watched the outcome of their attack. For some recently converted fledglings, this was the first time they had used their flame powers, so it was a big moment made bigger by the closeness of a feeding frenzy. Korbachev laughed and roared, showing his pleasure at the successful first strike.

"Now we feast!" he declared, causing much jubilation amongst his troops.

Inside the pub, there was instant panic. Those in the downstairs bar had only just recovered from the gruesome sight of Bernard South's death, and now the building was under attack - maybe even on the verge of collapse. The bar defenders were obviously about to take cover, but displaying once again the leadership skills which had enabled him to defeat the Gorakdezors, Edward kept a clear, cool head.

"Stay calm!" he ordered the others. "You panic; you play straight into their hands. Keep cool, maintain your positions, and wait for my order."

With a great deal of effort, he and PC Chandra managed to regain control over their makeshift battalion, and they all remained where they were, though Edward was sure he could hear Clyde Gillen whimpering. He could only hope the situation was under control upstairs.

No such luck. The restaurant was affected far more than the downstairs bar; the entire wall had crumbled away for a start. People were screaming and breaking cover, with Sarah, PC Scarlet and Emily trying frantically to reassert control. In the end, realising their strategy of hiding people upstairs had completely failed, Bob and Luke smashed open the back door and began evacuating people. Emily, Rossy and Scarlet remained behind with a few other brave souls, preparing to fight in order to buy the others time to escape.

In the attic, Emma was feeling conflicted. She was fully aware of the situation below and, with a good vantage point, she was thinking of opening fire upon the vampires. But this would give away her position and the vampires would probably attack her as well. Down below, hiding in hedges surrounding the pub, Amy, Beth, Sky and Tasia had the same problem - they could start shooting and help the others, but, exposed as they were, they would almost certainly die within minutes. As the girls all tried to make their own choices, Korbachev led the vampires in a charge, heading partly for the ruined side of the building, and partly for the shattered front window, which led straight into the bar where Edward's forces were lying in wait.

Seeing the vampires begin to turn to smoke and whirl upwards towards the restaurant floor, Edward made a decision. "Now!" he bellowed, and the twenty-strong force of concealed defenders broke cover and charged, blasting at the attackers with garlic cannons and hurling wine bottles and other projectiles. Chandra led the ragtag group forwards, a decision agreed by himself and Edward beforehand; Edward remained crouched where he was, firing with a garlic cannon at the supernatural intruders.

"Come on, get the bastards!" Chandra yelled, clobbering a vampire with his baton.

The sight rallied the defenders still further, and Clyde shoved the pointed end of a broken tableleg into the chest of another attacker. Poleaxed, the vampire gave a brief grunt of pain, and exploded into a cloud of ash. Nearby, David wrestled with another vampire until it too was hit with a garlic blast, knocking it screaming to the ground.

But the advantage was not held by the humans for long. As the fight raged, one stricken vampire lying in the road managed to sink its teeth into Clyde's leg as he ran past. Howling with pain, the young man sank to his knees, giving two nearby vampires an advantage which they gladly took - leaping onto Clyde's wiry frame and tearing him apart with their wicked fangs and claw-like fingernails. Chandra, too, was downed; as he struggled with one vampire, another approached quickly from behind and stabbed a small knife directly into the officer's jugular.

Gurgling desperately, the PC collapsed on the tarmac and drowned in his own blood.

From his hiding place, Edward swallowed. *That might have been me if we'd chosen our positions differently earlier,* he thought numbly.

The defenders were now in real trouble - with Chandra and Clyde dead, among others, the group was starting to fall apart. Some abandoned the fight and ran for it, trying to save themselves. David was nowhere to be seen, and Alex had been wounded - he staggered back into the bar, retreating to the only cover available.

Upstairs, things were even worse. In the short time that Edward's gang had been fighting Korbachev's foot soldiers, the man himself had wiped out most of the remaining people on the upper floor, with help from Rose and a few others. PC Scarlet had taken an opportunity to try and stab Korbachev in the back with a kitchen knife, but he was intercepted by Rose's hypnotic stare, and she then brutally turned his own weapon back on him. Emily and Rossy were forced back into the corridor by the force of the onslaught.

At roughly the same time downstairs, Edward grabbed a collapsed Alex and hauled him to his feet. The two made for a door behind the bar, which led to the stairs. As they passed the bar, Edward heard a familiar voice squeal his name, and glanced back to see Sophie hiding back behind the bar, minus her tableleg.

"Come on!" Edward yelled at his sister, before hurling himself through the door after Alex. After a beat, Sophie charged after them.

This was a mistake, as it was at that point that Korbachev, Rose and the other vampires on the top floor hurled more fireballs at the staircase, destroying the top of it in a blaze of fire. Emily and Rossy threw themselves down flat to protect themselves from the worst of the explosion, but down below, Edward, Sophie and Alex were completely unprepared for the resulting cascade of debris.

"Look out!" Edward managed to shout, a fraction of a second before the miniature avalanche smacked into the three of them, and everything went black.

* * *

Outside, the fleeing crowd of civilians had become a tidal wave of panicking, scrambling, desperate bodies, all trying to escape in any direction. They were easy pickings, and soon vampires were swooping down on the crowd. Many were quickly savaged by the attackers, but the vampires weren't the only problem. As Bob fought his way through the stampeding villagers, searching for Luke, he saw Clyde's girlfriend, Mae Hart, trip, fall and be almost immediately crushed underfoot by her own friends.

Bob shoved his way through to where Mae had fallen, knelt beside her and felt for a pulse - but there wasn't much point. Mae's head was surrounded in a growing pool of blood from her mouth and nose, her eyes were sightless, and her neck was twisted at an unnatural angle. Cursing, Bob struggled back to his feet, still fighting not to be knocked over by the crowd and share Mae's fate, and continued to search for Luke.

As he struggled on, he heard Sarah Blades screaming for them to stay calm. "We're only giving them what they want if we panic!" she was screeching frantically. "This is what they want!"

Yeah, and they're bloody getting it, Bob thought bleakly, as yet another civilian was plucked from the crowd and torn apart by a whirling cloud of black smoke.

* * *

Edward woke slowly, and realised gradually that his face was covered in dust. And that he was under a pile of rubble.

It took a moment for him to recall what had happened, and for his body to respond to the blinding pain in his foot. He acknowledged the agony with a short sharp grunt, and then focused on his surroundings. There was very little to see - it was almost pitch-black darkness, lit only by the raging fires through the gap in the nearby doorway, and what Edward could see did not fill him with hope. He was half-buried in the ruins of the staircase ceiling; loads of wood and plaster had tumbled down upon him, but by an unbelievable amount of luck he had not only escaped being crushed with barely any discernible injury - apart from his foot, which he could not see but felt sure had been split in half from the sheer pain - but also was able to wriggle out from under the rubble relatively easily. Once he had, he looked down at his foot to find the sole had been sliced open by a shard of glass.

Reaching into his toolbelt (*no Blade Runner should leave home without one*, he thought drily, before remembering that this was not the time to be making jokes), Edward took out his deep tissue scanner - an otherworldly medical device which allowed him to examine wounds even more closely by copying the wound on its screen and then digitally peeling back the layers of flesh, showing him what lay beneath the real wound - and quickly discovered the wound was entirely superficial, and no glass was stuck inside. Having covered the wound with a sterile dressing (also from the toolbelt) and replaced his damaged shoe, he stood up carefully and started scrabbling through the rubble, searching for Alex and Sophie.

A couple of minutes later, he had found both of them. The news was not good: Alex was dead, impaled on a wooden beam which must have been sheared in half to the point where it became basically a huge spear, and Sophie was unconscious but (according to the deep tissue scanner) unlikely to have any more severe injuries than concussion. He managed to haul her free, and after confirming that there was very little point trying to free Alex's body as well, he set about checking whether or not the staircase was still safe to use.

'Safe' is a loose term, Edward acknowledged. *This staircase can still be used, but I'd rather not risk it. I just hope everyone upstairs managed to escape before the thing got blasted.*

He crouched awkwardly in the rubble next to Sophie, who was now stirring feebly, and reloaded his garlic gun. *This is bad,* he thought. *We're getting brutalised out there - how can we possibly stand against this enemy?*

He forced himself to think rationally. *Come on: assets. What have we got here? Who can we contact elsewhere? Harold is at base, of course; I can get in touch with him with my radio. But is there anything at our base that can actually help?*

Edward thought for a minute, trying to remember all the pieces of alien tech they had, and feeling, not for the first time, grateful that he was autistic. *Is any of it of any use?*

Then it came to him.

He scrambled for his radio and spoke into it rapidly. "Venom to King One, are you receiving? Over."

After a few tense seconds of crackling static, Harold's reply came. "*King One receiving, Venom. What's the situation? Over.*"

"Listen to me, Harold, we don't have a lot of time. Have you finished analysing that Mekrashi Sun Force Globe? Over."

"*Er... yes, just now. Over.*"

"Good; I need you to bring it here. It might be our only chance of beating these guys."

* * *

Further up the ruined stairway, Emily was unconscious. Rossy knew this because the rubble had trapped him awkwardly close to her, his body pressed down on top of hers, and though he could feel her breath on his face, she had not stirred.

There came the sound of cruel laughter, which he recognised as belonging to Korbachev. A flash of red-hot anger surged through him.

"I've had enough of this," he spat.

With the slightest of willpower, he turned into smoke and slipped through the gaps in the rubble.

As he floated through the debris, he considered that the plan had been to go through a siege - and look how badly that had turned out. Many had died, and many more would die if the incursion was not halted. It was time to take the fight straight to the enemy.

* * *

Since the other Blade Runners had left, Harold had been manning the computers and phone lines for more vampire reports. Following Edward's new instruction though, he was packing weapons and the Mekrashi Sun Force Globe and preparing to set off for Pinchbeck.

He was almost ready when an indignant voice startled him.

"Where are you going?"

Kirsty had arrived at the Blade Runners' base about five and a half hours ago, and had been silent and immobile on the sofa for most of that time. She had been trying to process the events of that evening, and after introducing himself as 'King' (Kirsty did not recognise him even without his helmet on, because they had never met), Harold had left her to it. Now though, having decided she was not having a delusional episode, Kirsty was standing behind Harold, apparently fully alert.

"I need to go and help the others," Harold explained. "They need back-up - the vampires are all over them. You'll be safe here..."

Kirsty snorted. "Fat chance. I'm coming with you."

Harold looked alarmed. "No! It's too dangerous..."

"I can't sit here on my own any more! Your friends saved my skin; it's only fair I help them in return." There was a steely look in Kirsty's eyes, one which anyone who knew her would find unusual, which told Harold that this was non-negotiable.

He threw his hands in the air in frustration. "Fine. Just try not to get yourself killed."

As he stormed off, with a bag of weapons in one hand and the case containing the Sun Force Globe in the other, Kirsty hesitated before following, the steely look fading to be replaced by a look of anxiety and fear.

Maybe this wasn't such a good idea, she thought nervously. *I should stay here, where it's safe. That'd be the sensible thing.*

Then she grabbed a spare handgun from a nearby table and went after Harold.

Chapter 11

There were now fewer than thirty survivors left on the streets of Pinchbeck. The vampires were closing around them, and from where Bob was, things looked desperate. David was still nowhere in sight. Sarah was trying to keep the panicking survivors under control.

Above the action, Emma made a decision: she had watched too many people die, and her father and siblings might have been among them for all she knew. She couldn't leave it any longer - the remaining people below needed her help, and to hell with the consequences. She took aim with her crossbow, and was on the verge of firing when suddenly a barrage of bullets came out of nowhere at the vampire horde, killing dozens of them instantly. Emma flinched, confused: who had fired?

The answer came with a furious battle cry, as Cathy, Robbie and George charged out of the darkness, blasting at the vampires with machine guns. Taking this as a signal, Amy, Beth, Sky and Tasia opened fire from the hedges. David emerged from a nearby alley, shouting to Sarah, who led the survivors to the alley while the vampires were distracted by the Blade Runners' attack.

One vampire lunged out of the crowd, heading straight for the survivor group. Emma decided to take the opportunity and fired. Her aim was true, and the crossbow bolt speared the attacker through the throat. In the last moment before the vampire turned to dust, Emma recognised her as Ivy South.

In the street below, the vampires had been driven back significantly. Amy, Beth, Sky and Tasia had joined Cathy, Robbie and George in defensive positions around the survivor group. The ambush had taken no more than half a minute, but the Blade Runners now had the upper hand, and the survivors were finally escaping to - if not complete safety - at least somewhere less dangerous.

In the midst of the chaos Harold and Kirsty arrived, in a Blade Runner SUV. Sitting in the driver's seat, Harold observed the situation.

"Venom's not out here," he noted. "Probably still inside the Red Lion."

"If he isn't dead already," Kirsty pointed out bleakly, seeing the flames spewing out of the building.

Harold sighed. "Look, I should help the others, but I need to get this to Venom." He gestured to the case containing the Sun Force Globe. "You've got a handgun, so stay here and keep yourself safe while I go and find Venom. Understand?"

"Yeah, alright," Kirsty replied, after a moment's hesitation. "Except let's change that plan a bit: I'll go and find Venom in the dangerous burning building, and you stay outside and fight the murderous horde of vampires."

Harold frowned. "Surely you'd prefer to stay where it's safe?"

This suggestion was met with a burst of laughter. "Earlier tonight I was attacked in the Spar. Nowhere is safe at the moment. Besides, Venom saved me earlier; I just want to return the favour."

"Point taken. OK, I'll take the vampires; you take the burning pub."

*＊＊

Having clambered further up the ruined staircase and found Emily unconscious and trapped, Edward had managed to shift the rubble on top of her (with some considerable effort) and drag her free, before lying her down next to Sophie, who was still out cold. Thanks to the deep tissue scanner he knew Emily would be fine, but he needed back-up urgently or the building might decide to fall on them. Edward had radioed for back-up several times but there had been no reply; not even Harold was answering now.

He decided there was only one thing he could do: seek help elsewhere, which unfortunately meant he would have to leave Emily and Sophie for a few minutes at least. But what choice did he have?

Edward hauled himself to his feet - and a slender humanoid shape whirled screeching out of the darkness at him. He found himself struggling with a vampire girl, trying to keep her from sinking her fangs into his neck; the girl managed to overbalance him and send him tumbling forwards to the floor, hauling her down with him.

With both arms wrapped around the struggling girl, preventing her from moving, Edward couldn't grab any weapons, and as she wriggled like an eel, he knew he wouldn't be able to hold on for long. He also knew that in a second or two, she might think to turn into smoke, and then she would have the upper hand and he would be done for.

Then he heard running footsteps approaching, there was a thud and the vampire girl ceased her struggles. Edward looked up and observed several things in an instant: his assailant was Rose; his rescuer was Kirsty, the girl he had rescued from the Spar; Kirsty appeared to have just kicked Rose in the head; and Rose was not unconscious, simply dazed.

Moving faster than ever before (which, in his new occupation, was beginning to become a bit of a habit), Edward reached down and unsheathed his venom dagger. As Rose lunged at him again, he twisted out of her way and slashed her cheek with the blade, leaving a fine cut. Rose howled and lurched back, throwing herself back against the wall. Kirsty helped Edward get to his feet, and they faced the vampire.

"Don't try and fight us," Rose hissed, adopting a fighting stance. "Look how many people have been hurt, or killed, because you all tried to resist us. Just submit to Korbach-" She stopped suddenly, looking puzzled as her tongue stopped moving - quickly followed by the rest of her body. Rose was left standing frozen in front of Edward and Kirsty, looking like a confused, aggressive waxwork.

Kirsty looked just as bemused. "What's happened to her?"

Edward held up the dagger so she could see it. "There's venom in the blade; it paralyses its victims. When I slashed her cheek the venom entered her bloodstream; she's temporarily frozen."

"I thought vampires were basically dead? So their blood shouldn't move around their bodies any more?"

"That's a myth," he explained. "Harold checked that out for me on the database. Now, she's stuck like this for at least fifteen minutes, so we've got an opportunity to do something about her."

"We should kill her," Kirsty said. "She'd kill us if she had the chance."

Edward knew this would be the most sensible action. But could he bring himself to do it? This wasn't like killing Gorakdezors in human bodies, or even other vampires who had been human once. Rose was his friend; a girl he had been close to when he had lived in Kent. She was the same person now that she was then; Korbachev had just polluted her mind with all his dark ambitions. Could he really bring himself to kill her?

"Go on," Kirsty urged. "Otherwise she'll recover and she'll try and kill us again."

Edward sadly acknowledged that he couldn't really argue with that.

Feeling desperately unhappy, she stepped forwards and looked Rose directly in the eyes. They blazed with rage and hate, though the venom appeared to have disabled her hypnotic power. There was nothing left of the girl he had known in those eyes; just pure malevolence. The Rose he had been friends with was dead already - this was just an evil shadow.

He raised the dagger and thrust it forwards quickly. The point of the blade punched directly into her ribcage and stabbed deeply, slicing through her. There was an instant of terrible pain in her eyes, and her lips let the tiniest whimper escape - and then she exploded into a whirl of dust.

"Nice," Kirsty spluttered, coughing and flapping her hand in front of her face.

Edward said nothing. His eyes followed the particles of dust as they floated through the air - all that remained of Rose.

Kirsty moved closer. "You OK?"

"Not really," Edward replied in a hoarse whisper.

"You didn't want to do that, did you?"

Edward did not reply.

Kirsty took his hand and squeezed it, gently and reassuringly. "There wasn't another way, Venom."

He seemed to shake himself, to come out of his reverie. "Yeah," he said quietly. "You're right." He turned to face her. "And my name's Edward, by the way."

She laughed a little. "You were right; that's not as cool as 'Venom'."

"What are you doing here, anyway?"

"I wanted to help." Kirsty let go of his hand and walked over to a nearby heap of debris, on top of which was a large black case. "I brought you this."

Edward knelt down and undid the clasps on the case, before flipping the case open. He grinned at the sight of the contents.

"The Sun Force Globe," he whispered. "Now we've got a hope in hell."

Chapter 12

Korbachev was gloating. Rossy's blood boiled at the sight - the Russian vampire was standing in a garden opposite the Red Lion, surrounded by vampires, laughing at the violence around him. The building was still alight, with no chance of anyone being able to put out the flames, and the fight between the Blade Runners and the vampires was still raging furiously. Though the team's sudden attack had surprised the vampires, they were beginning to regain the upper hand, forcing the vigilantes back towards the burning pub.

As far as Rossy was concerned, if the snake's head was cut off, the body would die. If Korbachev was killed, the other vampires may lose their motivation and retreat. It was a slim hope, but at least it *was* a hope.

He crept out of hiding and turned into smoke, drifting quickly to the garden where Korbachev was watching the action. The vampire leader stood upon a ruined flowerbed, his hands on his hips, the epitome of victorious evil.

Turning solid once more, Rossy lunged forwards, screaming with righteous anger, images of his parents flashing through his minds, from photographs shown to him by his grandfather.

Korbachev didn't even look round. He simply flicked his wrist back, sending a dagger hidden up his sleeve flying at Rossy. It hit him right between the eyes, killing him instantly; his body exploded in a tornado of dust fragments, whirling across the garden.

Korbachev coughed slightly, and smiled. "Nice try, *vegan*. But Viktor Korbachev doesn't get taken down that easily."

"He does talk about himself in the third person though," said a voice from behind him. "And he does kill innocent, defenceless people."

This time he did turn around, intrigued by the new possible threat. What he saw confused even him: standing before him, caked in dried blood and unarmed, was the girl he had killed earlier - or someone very similar.

He took an involuntary step back. "How can you be... What *are* you?"

Lily - for, of course, it was she - stepped forwards, her eyes blazing. "I'm your worst nightmare, Korbachev. I'm one of your victims, back from the dead - to kill you."

The vampire leader felt himself fill with rage - and perhaps a hint of fear. "No," he roared. "You will not... I killed you once, I can do it again!"

And he threw himself at her, bellowing furiously.

She didn't even flinch. She stood there, never wavering, as the vampire hurled himself at her.

It's a trap, said a small voice in Korbachev's brain, but it was too late to acknowledge it.

Less than a second before he reached Lily, the bullet hit him in the head and blew his whole body apart, leaving a whirling cloud of ash.

She still didn't move. A few seconds later Nick reached her, holding a still-smoking sniper rifle.

"You OK?" he asked her softly, though he knew the answer already.

"I thought revenge would help," she replied bleakly, her face contorting with grief. "But it didn't. I felt nothing when he died; he just wasn't worth it."

She looked down her shirt, at her sister's dried blood.

"I've lost her," she whispered.

* * *

The Red Lion shuddered. Flames spewed from every door and window of the building, and further blasts of fire from the nearby vampire horde added to the furious inferno. The building clearly wasn't going to be left standing for much longer, but as long as it was, Edward still needed it.

He and Kirsty had left the pub a few minutes earlier and met Carter and Robbie coming the other way. With their help, they got Emily and Sophie out of the building, and just as they reached shelter in one of the Blade Runners' SUVs, the unconscious girls had started to come round.

"I have to go back in there," Edward had said to them. "The top of the building is the best vantage point, and Harold's told me how to use this" - here he held up the Sun Force Globe - "over the radios. If I get up there, I'll have a clear shot; I can take out every vampire for miles."

"Couldn't you just use another building?" Robbie had protested. "Going back in there would be ridiculously dangerous..."

Edward had gestured to the carnage around them. "I could try to get through this lot and get to another building, but even if I made it, it would be too late. This is quicker."

So, ignoring any further protests from his team, he had run back into the burning building, knowing the danger but also knowing the cost of doing nothing.

The staircase was still covered in rubble, but it was still possible to climb it. He passed the door leading to the upper restaurant: it was smashed off its hinges anyway, and he could see the fires burning furiously inside the room. Instead he headed up to the very top of the building, to the attic. The door was blocked by some of the rubble, but he managed to shift enough to open it a bit - just wide enough to squeeze through and into the room beyond.

The attic was not safe. Edward knew that as soon as he entered the room. The ceiling seemed on the verge of collapse, and smoke filled the room. Hand over mouth, he stepped through the gloom - and almost tripped over his sister.

"Emma!" he exclaimed, before going into a coughing fit. "Emma," he spluttered again, kneeling at her side. Thankfully she was still alive, and stirring feebly; the smoke must have made her pass out. He slapped her hard in the face, and she lurched into consciousness.

"Hey!" she protested. "What was that for?"

"I was *trying* to save your *life*," he told her hoarsely. "Now get out of here, and try not to knock the building down on your way out. I'm right behind you." He hauled her to her feet and pushed her in the direction of the door.

"Are you going to be OK?" she asked.

"I'll be fine! Now go!"

Reluctantly, Emma squeezed through the gap and vanished into the gloom of the staircase.

There was little time left: you didn't need to be a structure expert to know that this building was about to fall down. Edward raced to the open window and looked out and down, to see the Blade Runners and a handful of other humans clustered around the SUVs. The vampires were closing in around them, clearly about to make their final strike.

Quickly, he pulled the Sun Force Globe out of his pocket and started adjusting the dials and knobs on the side.

"Here goes everything," he muttered, and held the spherical weapon out of the window.

* * *

Emma had just run out of the Red Lion when a brilliant, dazzling light erupted above her. It was as if it was suddenly mid-day - the light poured down upon Pinchbeck, illuminating everything.

As one, the vampires screamed. As one, they tried to find cover from the light. As one, they failed. And every last vampire died, all of them disintegrating together in less than three seconds. The light remained until all of them were gone, and then vanished as if it had never been. Pinchbeck was dark once more.

The Blade Runners stopped shooting, lowering their assault rifles and looking around warily.

"They're gone," Cathy whispered.

"Edward must have used the Sun Force Globe," Harold told the rest of the group, before spotting Emma staggering away from the Red Lion.

"Emma!" Emily called, running over to her. "Are you alright?"

She nodded, too shocked by the sudden deaths of all the vampires to speak.

"Where's Edward?" Robbie asked urgently.

"He's still inside," she stammered.

"We need to get him out of there," Cathy declared.

And then the Red Lion finally collapsed, with a massive roar of fire. The last supporting parts of the structure finally gave way, and in the midst of an inferno the building was reduced to a heap of rubble. The Blade Runners ducked to avoid shrapnel from the explosion.

"No!" Emma shouted, trying to run back into the building, only for Cathy and Robbie to grab her and hold her back.

"You can't go in there," Cathy told her, struggling to keep the younger girl from breaking free. "You'll be killed."

"But what about Edward?" she cried, fear for her brother's life filling her eyes.

"What about him?" said a weary but slightly smug voice from behind them.

The Blade Runners whirled around, to find Edward, tired but triumphant, standing behind them, covered from head to toe in dust and soot. Emma rushed forwards to hug him, closely followed by Cathy. Robbie stepped forwards and gripped his hand happily, and the other Blade Runners moved in towards him in united joy.

"To be fair, that was quite a close one," he admitted. "Only managed to get out the back door about a second before the building fell down."

Kirsty moved through the group quickly, ducking and weaving until she reached Edward. He smiled at her. "You OK?" he asked.

"Yeah," she answered quietly, with a small smile. "I think I am."

And she kissed him.

For a moment he just stood there, stunned, as her lips pressed against his. He was trying to work out how to respond when she moved back, apologising.

"I shouldn't have..." she tried to say, looking embarrassed. "It's just a relief that it's over... Spur of the moment kind of thing... Sorry." Then she pushed back through the crowd and ran off.

For a few moments everyone was silent.

Then Harold frowned. "Where's the Sun Force Globe?"

Edward rolled his eyes. "Oh, I'll just pop back and get it, shall I?" he said sarcastically.

Harold laughed, and the rest of them started to join in, mainly just relieved and thankful that once again they had faced a seemingly unstoppable threat, and once again they had won.

Only Lily stood apart from the group, not joining in the celebration. Edward looked over at her, his laughter dying in his throat as he saw her blank, emotionless expression and limp demeanour. It was at that moment that he realised one of them was missing.

"Where's Abbie?" he asked.

Epilogue
Six Days Later

It felt unusually cold for the middle of May, and Edward shivered as he stood on the overgrown grass. Then again, he always felt cold in graveyards.

"Are you going to say anything?" Sophie asked quietly.

He shrugged. "What is there to say? The person she once was is gone - anything I could have said, I should have said when she was alive."

She frowned at him. "Well, I'm going to anyway, just in case," she told him, and knelt down by the gravestone.

"Abbie," she began. "I never met you, but I've heard about you. You were a really shy girl, but you were really clever. Apparently Edward gave you a hard time for not putting yourself in the action as much as the rest of his team, but he's sorry about that. I know he is."

Edward sighed, and looked around. The funeral had finished twenty minutes ago, but there were still people wandering the graveyard. David, Sarah and Emma had gone to talk to Abbie's mother, to pay their respects. The Blade Runners had all come to the funeral, and the others were sitting on the stone steps outside the graveyard, keeping Lily company.

There had been a lot to clear up after the battle - a lot of lives had been lost. It still wasn't clear just how many, because a fair few had been turned into vampires, so there would be nothing left of them. The Blades family may have survived intact, but others had not been so lucky - the Souths had lost their father and eldest child, and there were many others who had similarly suffered.

The official explanation for the night's events had been as suitably vague as the cover story Edward and his fellow Blade Runners had given for the Gorakdezor incursion - word had been put out by the villagers, on the advice of the Blade Runners, that violent street gangs had appeared in the night and ransacked houses, before smashing up and torching the Red Lion. The deaths had been explained away as murders by out-of-control hoodies as part of the gang attack. As for the Blade Runners, only those who had been at the Red Lion had learned their identities, and the survivors had agreed not to reveal them to the authorities, in gratitude for saving their lives.

Sophie was still talking to Abbie's gravestone. Laid in front of it were flowers, wreaths, cards, and all sorts of other mementoes from people who were close to her, and to her family.

"Lily's really sad that you died," Sophie was saying, "and so's your mummy. But they'll be OK in the end, because they know you're watching them. I hope heaven is nice, and I hope you're happy there."

Apparently finished, she stood up and went over to Edward.

"Are you all right?"

He hesitated before answering quietly. "I feel like this is my fault. I asked her to guard Rose, by herself. I should have stayed there and helped her; maybe she wouldn't have died..."

"It wasn't your fault," she told him. "That Korbachev guy killed Abbie. You saved all of us - everyone in Britain. I'm really proud of you."

He considered this for a moment, and then pulled her into a tight hug. "Yeah," he mumbled into her ear.

Cathy watched unnoticed from nearby.

***

"She's right, you know," Cathy told Edward, as they walked down the long, winding path to the graveyard gates. He frowned at her, not realising what she meant. "Sophie," she elaborated. "You didn't get Abbie killed, and you saved everyone. You can't beat yourself up over this."

"I know," he replied, though he still didn't sound sure. "It just felt like ever since the Gorakdezors, we're just losing more and more friends..."

"Be fair; we haven't lost anyone close *since* the Gorakdezors. And we were always going to lose people, Ed. I know the risks; so do you, and so do all the others. Abbie knew them too. We still joined you, though, because this job is worth the risks; worth the losses."

He looked at her; a deep, penetrating gaze. "You sure about that?"

"Yes," she said firmly. "Come on, we get to find out *what's out there*. Aliens and vampires and weird shit - who wouldn't want to be involved with that stuff? It's amazing and life-changing, and I wouldn't give it up for anything. I know you wouldn't either; it's like your dream come true."

He laughed a little. "Yeah. Or my favourite TV show come true."

They walked on in silence, thinking. After a few minutes, she spoke again. "What are you going to do now your family know what you're doing?"

"Carry on," he answered simply. "It's my life, and I chose this. If my parents don't like it, I'll move out."

"And are they OK with it?"

"Well, Mum isn't. Dad... Well, he's always a bit more laidback. But I think because he experienced it for himself... He'd never do what I do, but I think he understands why I do it." He massaged his temples with one hand. "I just wish they hadn't got involved... They'd be better off not knowing what's going on."

"Bit late for that," she pointed out.

"Yeah," he agreed. "I'll just have to make sure they don't get caught up in things in future."

* * *

Edward and Cathy walked through the graveyard gates together. A world of madness, of wild creatures and terrible evils, awaited them and their friends.

There was a rustle of leaves as a dishevelled figure stepped out from behind the gnarled, ancient tree standing near the gates. The figure watched as Edward and Cathy walked out of sight.

It was a young man, no older than twenty. His hair was overgrown and flopped down in front of his eyes; the lower half of his face was covered by a beard; and he wore a grey hoodie.

The man let a low growl escape the pit of his throat - and then let out a brief, angry bark of rage. And 'bark' was literal: he sounded exactly like a dog.

Then he turned, crouched, and ran on all fours into the maze of gravestones.

COMING SOON:
OUTCAST

Edward is back, and this time, he's on his own.

Everyone around him has turned against him. Angry mobs are around every corner, and even those closest to him do not trust him.

Edward has always relied on his friends - so how can he survive when they become his enemies?